STRANGER AND STRANGER

It seemed impossiut it
had.

It was unthinkable ut it
was.

Diana had time to move when he moved his horse
closer, she really did. And she could have used her riding crop to push him away. Instead, she sat very still and
waited as he did what he had done so startlingly and
shockingly before. But this time she was not in the least
surprised when his free arm went around her and his lips
closed over hers. And this time his kiss was gentle, seductive, teasing. He nibbled at her lower lip, his tongue
danced over the corners of her mouth. When her lips
parted as if they had a will of their own, his tongue
darted inside, unable to resist the invitation. And when
he pulled her still closer, his embrace more demanding,
she didn't resist.

Diana was in the clutches of a total stranger. But even
stranger was the way he made her feel.

SIGNET REGENCY ROMANCE
Coming in May 1996

Evelyn Richardson
The Reluctant Heiress

Patricia Oliver
The Colonel's Lady

Emma Lange
The Irish Rake

Barbara Allister
The Frustrated Bridegroom

The Wicked Groom

April Kihlstrom

A SIGNET BOOK

SIGNET
Published by the Penguin Group
Penguin Books USA Inc., 375 Hudson Street,
New York, New York 10014, U.S.A.
Penguin Books Ltd, 27 Wrights Lane,
London W8 5TZ, England
Penguin Books Australia Ltd, Ringwood,
Victoria, Australia
Penguin Books Canada Ltd, 10 Alcorn Avenue,
Toronto, Ontario, Canada M4V 3B2
Penguin Books (N.Z.) Ltd, 182–190 Wairau Road,
Auckland 10, New Zealand

Penguin Books Ltd, Registered Offices:
Harmondsworth, Middlesex, England

First Printing, April, 1996
10 9 8 7 6 5 4 3 2 1

Copyright © April Kihlstrom, 1996
All rights reserved

Prologue

It was the Duchess of Berenford who sowed the seeds of the disaster. She hadn't meant to, but she couldn't help herself. It all happened shortly after her son, the Duke of Berenford, proposed marriage to a woman he had never seen. Less than three weeks later, the Duchess of Berenford sat in her elegantly appointed, old fashioned drawing room in London and frowned at her son.

"I fail to comprehend your distress," the Duchess of Berenford said impatiently. "You have become engaged to an eminently suitable young lady who will do justice to the Berenford family. Her lineage is almost as good as your own, her breeding impeccable, and her countenance is said to be exquisite. What more could you ask for, Jeremy?"

The ninth Duke of Berenford regarded his mother bleakly. "Love," he said succinctly.

"Love?" The duchess snorted contemptuously. "Nonsense! You will get along very much better without it. Trust me in this, for I have good reason to know. My sister married for love, and where has it gotten her?"

Berenford winced, but did not say the words on his mind; that his aunt had always seemed a far happier person to him than his own mother, despite the fact that one enjoyed all the advantages of wealth and privilege, and the other scraped along as the impoverished wife of a vicar.

Apparently, silence was not enough to satisfy his mother. The duchess thumped her cane against the floor as she demanded, "Well? Do you mean to moon about from now until your wedding day and after? Your bride will not be pleased if you greet her with just such a Friday face as this at the breakfast table each morning."

"And just how should I greet her?" Berenford asked ironically.

"With politeness, just as she shall greet you," the duchess replied austerely. She paused, then asked, a trifle more gently, "What the devil is the matter with you, Jeremy? You agreed to this match of your own free will."

"Oh, yes, I agreed," Jeremy said in the same ironical tone as before. "Why not? I must marry someone, and, as you say, the Lady Diana is lovely, well bred, and has a suitable lineage. It's just that I don't know her."

"Don't know her? Of course you don't know her," the duchess said, increasingly impatient. "She's been properly raised at home, and her father's kept her there. As I understand it, she didn't want to go anywhere else. No nonsense of wanting to spend all her time in London, which you wouldn't want, either. It's one of the reasons I chose her for you. She'll be perfect. But if you must get to know her before the wedding, why not go for a visit? Her family will welcome you with open arms, I assure you."

Jeremy regarded his mother with an oddly affectionate smile. What would his mother say if she knew he had already been invited and declined? His mother meant well, he knew it, and yet she simply did not understand.

Berenford sighed and tried to explain. "I don't want to simply meet the girl, Mother. I want to get to know her, to see what kind of wife she will make, in bad times as well as good. If I go for a formal visit, it will all be so stuffily proper with scarcely a moment alone between us and nothing said to the point. We will both be on our best behavior and probably bore each other to death."

The Duchess of Berenford rolled her eyes. "Well, what on earth do you expect?" she demanded. "It's all I knew of your father before we were wed. And we rubbed along well enough together afterward. No one knows their betrothed before the wedding. The only ones who ever see another person as he or she really is are servants, and any servant of Lady Diana's will be far too loyal to speak of her to you. No, accept it, my boy. Your romantic notions are all very well in books, though I scarcely waste my time on such things, but in real life one must be practical. You need a wife, and Lady Diana will suit. For romance you need simply look discreetly elsewhere whenever you wish. Lady Diana's been properly brought up. She won't raise a fuss. Not so long as you are discreet about the matter, and I've certainly brought you up to be that."

The Duke of Berenford held his breath throughout this speech and then let it out. There was no point in arguing with his mother. She was stubborn to a fault and thought him cork-brained over this matter. No, he would have to resolve it himself. Something she said began to work its way through his brain, however—a servant. The only ones who saw members of the gentry as they really were, were the servants. But for the moment, Berenford set the thought aside and turned his attention to charming his mother over tea.

* * *

Meanwhile, in another part of England, the Countess of Westcott, a very pretty and petite woman, regarded her husband with some concern. "I don't understand it, Adam," she said unhappily. "How could the Duke of Berenford turn down our invitation to visit?"

The Earl of Westcott shifted uneasily in his chair. It was most unlike his wife to accost him here, in the library, a room that had been his refuge during the past twenty-one years of their marriage. "Well, my dear, you see for yourself," he said, indicating the letter she held, "the Duke of Berenford has other, pressing engagements."

The countess snorted a most unladylike snort. "Nonsense! Berenford could come and see his bride-to-be if he wished. Anyone would understand."

"Perhaps he doesn't want to see Diana before the wedding," Westcott suggested. "P'rhaps he's superstitious. Thinks it would be bad luck to see her beforehand."

"In short, he's as reluctant for the match as Diana?" the Countess of Westcott asked shrewdly. "You may be right. I just hope he doesn't cry off before we get them to the altar. This may be our only chance to get Diana off our hands, you know."

The Earl of Westcott looked at his wife nervously. "P'rhaps this wasn't such a good notion," he said. "Mean to say, if they're both so reluctant . . ."

His voice trailed off as his wife glared at him. The countess began to pace back and forth. "Nonsense!" she repeated. "It's a good match. Suitable for both of them. And if they're both reluctant, so much the better. He won't come pestering Diana more often than he must. And that will be a blessing, even if she doesn't know it yet. That's one of the reasons I chose Berenford for her. He has the reputation of being a cold man. And since Diana's never shown the least interest in the young men hereabouts, I cannot think she would want an ardent lover for a husband. Diana will do far better with a man who does not expect frequent displays of affection from her. She should be grateful for the consideration I've shown in choosing Berenford for her. But is she? Not in the least."

Westcott blanched at these words. They conjured up in his mind a clear image of the past twenty-one years and the way his wife had always gritted her teeth as she did her duty by him. She'd done it often enough to present him with five daughters, he had to give her that, and yet there had been no joy in their joining. Was he a fool to wish there had been? So far as Westcott could tell by listening to his peers, most marriages were like his. That was why so many men had mistresses.

And yet, Westcott had hoped for more for his daughters—particularly for Diana, who was his favorite. Westcott had hoped that Berenford, given his many mistresses over the years, could teach Diana to find joy in fulfilling her wedding vows. But now Lady Westcott's words put another face upon the matter. Except for one instance, some years ago, that had ended badly, Berenford had always avoided the round of balls and routs and such that made up the Season and disdained to favor any girl with his attentions. Suppose he continued this coolness with Diana and never made any attempt to teach her the pleasures of the marriage bed? Suppose he intended to continue to carry on with his mistress? Diana was a proud girl. She wouldn't like that. She wouldn't like that at all.

The Earl of Westcott abruptly reversed himself and said,

cutting his wife off in mid-sentence, "Very well, I shall write the Duke of Berenford again and try to persuade him to visit."

Lady Westcott hadn't the slightest notion why her husband had done such an about-face, but she wasn't inclined to argue. It was fortunate for her peace of mind that she had no idea what was about to occur.

Chapter One

~

The Lady Diana paced about the stable yard impatiently as she waited for her horse to be brought out. Mama had been lecturing her, once again, and Diana was impatient to be gone. She wanted to race her horse across the fields and ride off some of her restlessness.

After what seemed an eternity, a groom appeared, leading two horses. "What are you doing?" Diana demanded, pointing past her own mare, Lucky Lady, toward the other horse.

Rawlins, the head groom, hastily answered, "Your father's orders, my lady. Now that you're to be married, he said you must always take a groom with you when you go out riding."

Diana's lips set in a grim line Rawlins recognized only too well. "I won't have it," she said in a dangerously quiet voice.

"You will, my lady, or you won't go riding at all," Rawlins replied in no uncertain terms.

The Lady Diana stared at Rawlins, and he met her gaze without flinching. After a moment she sighed. From years of experience she knew that once Rawlins had been given his orders, he would carry them out, whatever she might say to the contrary. Through clenched teeth Diana said, "Very well, but whoever comes with me had better be able to ride."

"As if I'd have grooms who couldn't," Rawlins retorted indignantly.

Now the other groom spoke hesitantly, almost meekly, Diana thought disdainfully. "I can ride, m'lady," he said, "powerful well."

"That we shall see," Diana countered bluntly.

Diana allowed Rawlins to boost her into the saddle, and then she urged Lucky Lady to canter out of the stable yard, not looking behind her to see if the groom was ready. If he wasn't, that was his lookout. She didn't want an escort in the first place.

Diana rode hard, giving Lucky Lady her head. They both wanted, after all, to reach the same destination. There was a brook on her father's land and a shaded spot by the brook where she could be alone. Except, of course, for that absurd groom Rawlins had saddled her with. Who the devil was he, anyway? Diana could not recall seeing him about before this.

Abruptly, she pulled Lucky Lady up short and looked back, expecting to see the groom laboring far behind her. Instead, she saw him almost at her shoulder. She hadn't paid attention in the stable yard, noting only that another horse had been saddled, but now Diana realized the groom was riding one of her father's best horses and seemed to have no difficulty controlling the beast.

"Father never lets anyone ride Devil except himself," she said inconsequentially.

The groom started to smile, then seemed to think better of it. Instead, he kept his eyes on the ground and answered meekly, "Rawlins seemed to think Devil needed the exercise and that I would need Devil to keep up with you, m'lady. From the past few minutes, I'd say he had the right of it."

Was that impertinence? Diana frowned. "What is your name?" she asked sharply.

"J-James, m'lady," the poor man stuttered.

"I don't think I've seen you about before," Diana persisted.

"Aye, you've the right of it," James agreed. "I'm a new one here. Rawlins hired me yesterday afternoon."

Diana's clear blue eyes widened in surprise. "And he trusted you with Devil already?"

James shrugged, clearly embarrassed. "Yes, well, m'lady," he said, clearing his throat, "there was some trouble with Devil just last night, and, well, seemed to be I was the only one who could control him."

"Are you a gypsy?" Diana demanded abruptly.

Now the groom stared at her, clearly startled by the question. "No, m'lady," he replied, as though affronted.

To her utter astonishment, Lady Diana found herself apologizing. "I meant no offense or insult, James," she said. "It's just that I've heard tales of how gypsies often have a special way with animals, and you must be very good if you were able to calm Devil."

Now the groom's broad shoulders relaxed, and a smile did touch his eyes, if not his lips, as he replied, "No offense taken, my lady."

For some reason his amusement angered Diana. She didn't like to be in the wrong. Curtly, she said, "Yes, well, you'd best learn to curb that temper of yours. It won't do to be brawling in the stables. Rawlins will turn you off without a reference if you do."

"Temper?" James repeated evenly. "It wasn't temper you

saw in my face, m'lady," he told her. "It was merely surprise. No one's called me a gypsy before, is all."

That made Diana even angrier. Without another word she turned and urged Lucky Lady to gallop across the last remaining field to the brook. This time she didn't expect to outrun the groom. Neither, however, did she expect him to put his hands on her to help her down from her horse.

"Here, m'lady, let me help you," he said just before he placed his hands on her hips and lifted Diana down to the ground.

The moment her feet touched earth, Diana threw off her shock and shoved hard against the groom's chest. "Let go of me!" she shrieked. "You are never to touch me again, do you hear?"

The groom blinked, then a slow smile spread across his face. "Begging your pardon, my lady," he said. "I mistook my place. I only wanted to help you. And begging your pardon, my lady, but if my touch makes you so skittish, how are you going to bear being married, as they say you will be soon? Your husband will touch you a sight more than that."

Diana wanted to strike the groom. Instead, her eyes widened. His words struck a tender spot, and she hastily turned away so he would not see her turmoil. "That is none of your affair," she said as frigidly as possible.

Behind her the groom frowned. His brows were pulled together in a puzzled furrow, and he almost spoke. Perhaps it was the thought of being sent off without a character that kept him silent instead.

After a moment Diana seemed to visibly draw herself together again. She turned to face James and took a deep breath before she spoke. In a voice that was cool and distant, but not unfriendly, she said, "Forgive me. It is not your fault if you have not been sufficiently well trained. In the future, however, I shall expect you to remember that if I require assistance, I shall request it, and otherwise you are not to touch me. Is that clear?"

"Perfectly, my lady," James replied meekly.

Diana nodded curtly. "Good. You may tether the horses over there or walk them if you wish. I intend to sit by the stream for a bit, and I don't wish to engage in useless conversation."

It was a dismissal, and James should have taken it as one. Perversely, however, the grin crept back into his eyes and tugged at the corners of his mouth again. "Begging your pardon, m'lady," he told her, "but I can't imagine anything you say being useless."

Diana was not deceived by the meekness of his tone. Exasperation was in her voice as she replied, but something else as well, perhaps a hint of laughter. "I wasn't talking about *my* conversation," she said, "I was referring to yours. Not," Diana added with a melancholy edge to her voice and a wistful look in her eyes, "that mine is always to the point. Sometimes I think I shall never learn to speak as I should. Mama despairs of bringing me up to scratch before my betrothed, Lord Berenford, comes to meet me. And I quite frankly dread the moment he does."

The groom frowned. "Is he such a fearsome fellow, then, this Lord Beremord?" James asked ingenuously.

Diana smiled wistfully. It was absurd to be confiding in a groom this way, but somehow she couldn't help herself. Perhaps it was because he was just a servant—someone who wouldn't think to tell Mama or Papa what she had said.

"It's Lord Berenford," she corrected him automatically. "And I don't know if he's fearsome. He's probably some fashionable popinjay. It's just that I know Berenford won't like me as I am. He'll try to turn me into a society wife, and I shall hate it thoroughly."

"Then you mustn't let him do so," James said promptly. More seriously, he asked, "Why marry him if that's how you feel?"

Diana sighed and turned away, unwilling to have the groom see all her emotions reflected in her eyes. "I'm the eldest. I must marry sometime. I must marry well. Why not marry Lord Berenford? He's suitable, and both families are pleased with the match."

"Aye, but what about you and he?" James asked roughly.

Now Diana turned and looked at him. She shook her head gently. "You don't understand what it's like for us, for the gentry. You can marry as you wish, but we must marry with all sorts of other considerations in mind." Then forcing a bright note into her voice, she added, "I expect it will all turn out very well. This sort of marriage often does, you know. It is just missishness on my part to feel as I do. Perhaps once I meet Lord Berenford, I shall fall madly in love with him and live happily ever after."

James snorted. Still, there was a disturbing hint of laughter in his eyes as he said, "What if he's eighty and subject to gout?"

"Oh, no," Diana assured him earnestly. "I have it on the best authority that Lord Berenford is young and quite handsome."

"Is he?" James said, apparently impressed. Some devilish impulse made him add, "Are you looking forward to kissing him, then?"

Diana blinked in astonishment. An instant later, her voice was coldly repressive as she said, "You go too far, James."

"Oh, no," was his soft reply. "*This* is too far."

And then he kissed her. James took Diana by surprise, and the kiss was planted before she even had time to react. When she did, she slapped his face, whirled to where Lucky Lady stood waiting, and used a nearby rock to hastily mount the mare. Then she was riding like the wind as far and as fast as she could go to get away from him.

With a chuckle James mounted his own horse and set Devil flying after his mistress. He was scarcely a length behind by the time they reached the stable yard. The mark on his face from her hand had already faded, but nothing could conceal the fact that Lady Diana's hair had escaped from all of its pins. The moment Lucky Lady came to a halt in front of Rawlins, Diana slid from her mare's back.

"I want him fired!" Diana said, pointing to James. "Immediately. I want him turned off without a character."

"Oh, and why is that?" Rawlins asked easily.

"He tried to take liberties with me!" Diana said, her eyes full of rage.

To Diana's utter astonishment, Rawlins chuckled and shook his head. "Sorry, Miss Diana. Your father said you would say something of the sort if the groom I picked was able to keep up with you. Now you just settle down and accept being a betrothed young lady who must begin to act like one. Seems to me that James was right on your heels, just as he was supposed to be, and that's what's setting up your back. Which means he's just the one to send out with you again."

Rawlins turned to the groom, who had also slid off his horse and come to stand beside them. "Good work, James," Rawlins said. "Mind, now, you're to keep watch. And if Miss Diana, Lady Diana, that is, wishes to go riding, you're to accompany her, all right?"

"Yes, sir," James said meekly.

"Aye, and don't mind if you've been given other chores to do," Rawlins added sternly. "Lady Diana comes before all else."

Again James nodded meekly, deceiving Diana not in the least. As rage threatened to overwhelm her, Diana turned on her heel and started toward the house. If Rawlins would not listen to reason, then perhaps her father would. He couldn't seriously intend for her to put up with the impertinence of a groom! Behind her, it was infuriating to hear Rawlins chuckling once more and giving James advice on how to handle her. If Diana had had a pistol handy, she thought she would have put a shot through both of them.

Chapter Two

∼

Diana stormed into the foyer of the house. Her gloves, hat, and riding crop were tossed carelessly onto a table, and the footman had to leap to catch them from falling onto the floor.

"Where is my father?" she demanded imperiously.

"In the library, I believe, my lady," the hapless footman stuttered, relieved that her anger did not seem to be focused on him.

Diana marched down the hallway toward the library. She cursed the long skirt of her hunter green habit that kept threatening to trip her up, and finally she looped it scandalously high over her wrist so that she could march unimpeded. She entered the library without knocking, throwing open the door with great force, and marched straight up to her father's desk.

"Why must I be married?" Diana demanded without preamble.

The Earl of Westcott leaned back in his chair, unperturbed by his daughter's extraordinary behavior. But then, for Diana, it was more ordinary than not. "You know very well why you must be married, Diana," he said calmly. "You are the eldest, and there are four sisters to come after you. Annabelle is already all but pledged to Winsborough, and she cannot marry until after you have done so."

Diana began to pace about the room. "Why?" she demanded. "Why can't Annabelle go first?"

"Because that is not the way things work," Westcott replied calmly. "Really, Diana, I don't understand these histrionics. You agreed to marry the Duke of Berenford, and I fail to see why you should suddenly cavil at the match now. Has someone been feeding you lies about the fellow? Have you heard something to his detriment? Because I tell you frankly, I have not, and I have made it my business to learn all I can about the fellow." Westcott paused, then added sternly, "Recollect, Diana, that I did offer to send you to London for a Season. If you had gone, you could have made your own choice of a spouse."

Diana paused in her pacing to shake her head impatiently. "It's not Berenford," she said. "I just don't want to be married at all. I've been thinking, you see, and I realize I don't want a husband looking after me."

The Earl of Westcott sighed. "All right," he said. "Tell me what's happened to overset you like this."

"You, Papa," Diana replied bluntly. "You've overset me. You've given orders that I'm no longer to be allowed to ride Lucky Lady alone. I'm to have a groom ride with me. And Mama is even worse. She says I must be fitted for all sorts of clothes. More clothes than I shall ever need in a lifetime. If I had known that this was the sort of nonsense my betrothal would bring, I would never have agreed to it in the first place."

This last was said with patent anguish, and because he loved his daughter, the Earl of Westcott winced. "I'm sorry, my girl," he said softly. "We're trying only to help you get ready for your marriage. Things will change. And I can't deny that some of the changes you will dislike. But there are other changes you may heartily approve of."

Diana strode to her father's desk and planted her hands on it while she leaned forward and demanded, "Will I? Precisely what changes will I approve of, Father?"

The earl did not answer. He could not. Instead, he muttered, half to himself. "I wish Berenford had decided to come and visit you. He's said to be a charming fellow, and that might have been enough to outweigh your fears."

Diana snorted, causing her father to shudder with the realization of just how unladylike his daughter could sound. "I'm not a fool," she said, "to be distracted by a pretty face or a charming smile. The only reason I agreed to marry Berenford is because you assured me he has a mind. But if he does, I haven't seen any sign of it. Or perhaps he's as reluctant for this match as I am, and would be relieved if I called it off."

The Earl of Westcott regarded his daughter in horror. "No! Good God, you mustn't even think such a thing!" he protested. "If either of you cried off now, you would both be ruined."

Again Diana snorted. "Don't be a fool, Papa," she said impatiently. "I am the daughter of an earl with an ample dowry. I could have a scar running down my face, run off with a groom, and still find a husband if I wished. As for Berenford, nothing will scare off Mamas looking for wealthy, titled husbands for their cherished daughters."

"Nevertheless, I will not have you disgrace the family," Westcott said implacably. "You have made a bargain, and I expect you to keep it."

For a moment matters hung in the balance. Then Diana turned neatly on her heel and strode out of the room, her head and chin held high. She would not cry, she told herself with grim determination. No matter what happened, she would not cry.

Upstairs, Diana's resolve might have crumbled save for the fact that her sisters were waiting to pounce upon her the moment she entered the nursery to see them.

Diana paused on the threshold, her ill humor dissolving as she stared at the picture her four sisters made. Annabelle was closest in age to her at seventeen; Barbara came next at sixteen; and then came the twins, Rebecca and Penelope, at fourteen. Four more different girls could scarcely have been found. Their color ranged from Diana's own pale blond locks and startling blue eyes to Barbara's dark hair and amber eyes with the others all in between. And yet they were close. Particularly at the moment, for the most recent governess had fled the scene after an especially atrocious prank played by the twins, involving spiders in the poor woman's bed.

Still, of them all, Diana felt closet to Barbara. She was as wild as Diana and often worried her older sister. The others were more amenable, and Diana cared for them so much that sometimes she felt more like their mother than their sister. That was why she had agreed to marry, of course. Whatever the sacrifice on her part, she could not stand in the way of her sisters' finding happiness.

Now they greeted her with knowing grins. "You've been in a temper, haven't you?" Rebecca said shrewdly.

Annabelle groaned. "Not another fight with Mama, I hope?"

Diana stepped into the room, careful to keep her voice light as she replied, "No, with Papa this time. I decided it was his turn, after all."

"Oh, Diana," Annabelle sighed helplessly.

"Fustian!" Barbara exclaimed roundly. "If Diana fought

with Papa, she had good reason. We all ought to fight more with Mama and Papa. Then we would get what we want."

"But Mama and Papa give us everything," Rebecca protested. "Why should we fight for more?"

Barbara and Diana exchanged speaking glances. Still, there was no point in upsetting the other girls any further. Diana smiled brightly and said, "Yes, well, it's all blown over, so you've nothing to worry about. Papa knows my temper too well to take anything I say seriously."

That prompted a hastily muffled snort of laughter from Penelope. "We all know your temper very well," she said sardonically. "What set you off this time?"

Diana gripped her hands tightly together as she replied, again with the same light tone as before, "Oh, all these rules Papa and Mama have imposed on me, now that I have become betrothed to the Duke of Berenford. Do you know that I am not even to go riding without a groom?"

"Considering that you ride neck or nothing, it isn't a bad notion, betrothed or not," Annabelle said severely.

Diana cast an indulgent smile toward her younger sister, but it was Barbara who asked the shrewdest question. "And was it the rule or the groom you took exception to?" Barbara demanded, eyeing her sister closely.

Diana hesitated. "Both," she said with uncharacteristic uncertainty.

"Who did Rawlins send out with you?" Annabelle asked, frowning. "I thought none of the grooms could keep up with you and Lucky Lady."

Now Diana bit her lower lip in an even more uncharacteristic gesture. Finally, she answered reluctantly, "Rawlins found a new groom. His name is James, and I don't like him. I don't like him at all. He was . . . impertinent."

Diana's sisters looked at one another and grinned know-

ingly. "That means he *did* keep up with you," Penelope said
with a grown-up air.

"And that means Rawlins will send him out with you
every time," Rebecca added breathlessly.

"It serves you right if he's impertinent," Annabelle
added severely, though there was an understanding twinkle
in her eyes as well. "If you hadn't frightened every other
groom on the estate, Rawlins could have sent someone
properly deferential to attend you."

Only Barbara seemed to understand. She set down the
book she had been reading, came over to Diana, and placed
a hand on her arm. "Is he truly that bad?" she asked sympathetically.

That bad? The question sent an odd sensation through
Diana, for she suddenly realized he wasn't that bad. Indeed,
the trouble was, she didn't think James was bad at all. She
had liked his kiss, and that frightened her most of all. But
Barbara was waiting for an answer, and Diana had to say
something. She forced a smile and said, "Oh, I suppose not.
I just chafe at all these restrictions."

Barbara squeezed her arm again in sympathy, and Diana
felt like a fraud. But what could she say? That she'd kissed
a groom and liked it? Barbara would understand, but her
other sisters would be scandalized, and if anyone else found
out, it would put her beyond the pale. So now Diana swung
around and said, "All right, who's got the fashion book?
I've got to start thinking of my trousseau."

In the doorway of the room Lady Westcott paused to
look over her children. Undeniably, there was a great deal
to be proud of. Nevertheless, Lady Westcott worried. Her
daughters had run far too wild for far too long, and she
knew it. Look at them! she thought. Diana in her shabby,
out-of-date riding habit, Barbara outgrowing her gown al-

ready, the twins with torn hems, and only Annabelle dressed as she ought to be in a print muslin morning gown. Something must be done! Never one to shirk a task, Lady Westcott straightened her shoulders and entered the room.

"I can see that it is time and past that I replaced your governess. Perhaps you will show a more proper decorum when Miss Tibbles, the governess my sister is sending up from London, arrives," Lady Westcott said as she watched the twins tumble off the window seat.

The five sisters looked at one another with some trepidation. To be sure, both Diana and Annabelle had already left the schoolroom; nevertheless, even they would be affected by this new development. No longer would it be possible to have a comfortable coze with their sisters in the nursery, not with this Miss Tibbles expecting the younger girls to be at their lessons. As for Barbara, there was a distinctly martial gleam in her eyes that betokened trouble.

"You will show Miss Tibbles the respect that is her proper due when she arrives," Lady Westcott said, bending a particularly stern eye on her third eldest daughter.

"When does Miss Tibbles arrive?" Penelope asked ingenuously.

Lady Westcott considered her young daughter for a long moment before she replied thoughtfully, "I don't think I shall tell you. I wouldn't want you to have any warning if you were thinking, any of you, of behaving in an untoward manner. I will not have you pulling the sorts of pranks that have driven away your last six governesses." She paused and smiled what her daughters considered to be a distinctly wicked smile, then added, "My sister assures me, however, that I needn't worry. Miss Tibbles will be quite up to your tricks and perfectly capable of taking you all in hand."

* * *

In the stable the newest groom was busy rubbing down and brushing both Lucky Lady and Devil. Rawlins eyed him thoughtfully for several minutes. There was nothing to fault in his manner with the horses, and of course he didn't believe Lady Diana's outrageous charges, but still, it wouldn't hurt to drop a word in the fellow's ear.

Rawlins strolled closer to James. "Bit of a handful, Lady Diana is," he observed carelessly.

James did not stop his work or turn around. "Aye, that she be," he said.

"Indulged by her papa, she's been," Rawlins added. "The earl always did want a son."

"Guessed it, I did," James replied, brushing harder. "Rare bruising rider she is. Had my hands full, keeping up with her."

"That's all you did, isn't it? Keep up with her?" Rawlins asked.

James slowly turned around. There was exasperation in his face and in his voice as he replied, "Now and what would I be wanting with a termagant like that? A soft, sweet armful, mayhap, but even then I'd not risk losing my job over a pair of eyes."

Rawlins nodded, but his own eyes narrowed thoughtfully. Sure and what was a groom doing using words like termagant? Still, so long as the man did his job, it made no difference to Rawlins if he talked above himself. And he did have a way with horses.

"Devil give you any trouble?" Rawlins asked, changing the subject abruptly.

Now James grinned. "Not once we'd settled who was going to control the reins," he said. "A right powerful horse, he is, and one I'd not mind owning meself."

At that Rawlins snorted. "Horses like Devil are not for

the likes of you and me," he said with a laugh. "Except for grooming and riding for someone else. Why the tax alone is more than you or I make in a year."

James seemed to bridle at that. "A feller can dream, can't he?" he demanded.

Rawlins chuckled again. "Oh, aye, dreams! Dream away, lad, but don't get so far above yourself you forget they're dreams."

"I won't," James promised, but there was a hint of determination at the back of his eyes, and Rawlins felt the first twinge of alarm.

"You aren't dreaming any dreams about Lady Diana, are you?" Rawlins asked sharply.

"The only skirts I dream about," James answered easily, "are those I knows I can have."

Rawlins breathed a sigh of relief. "That's all right then," he said, half to himself. "Very well. When you finish here, I'll need you to rake out the rest of the stalls."

"Aye, Mr. Rawlins," James said, touching his cap.

Something made Rawlins hesitate and add, "Seems a pity to waste you on that, seeing the touch you have with the horses, but the rest, they'd not understand if I left the new groom off the chore of mucking out."

"I don't mind," James said with a shrug.

Somewhat to his surprise, Rawlins realized the fellow didn't.

Chapter Three

~

Two days later, Lady Diana approached the stables war-ily. She had tried not going there, but it hadn't worked. She missed Lucky Lady. Diana missed riding—galloping with her hair flowing free behind her and the wind in her face. She would just ignore the groom, James, and not allow him the opportunity to be impertinent to her again, Diana told herself. Surely, she could do that. She need only make certain she did not dismount while he was around. She could walk out to the stream, later, if she wished, to sit and think. For now Diana wanted to ride.

The moment Rawlins saw her coming, he sent James in-side to ready the horses. Once again Diana found both Lucky Lady and Devil saddled and ready. Her lips tight-ened into a narrow line, but she did not protest. Her father often said that winning a war meant knowing which battles to fight and which to let go by.

Still, the moment Rawlins tossed her up into the saddle, Diana was off, noting with glee from the corner of her eye that James had not yet settled onto Devil. Let him run to catch her! She might have to accept his company, but even her father would know better than to expect her to make it easy for the fellow. If he couldn't keep up, perhaps they would fire him.

When, after half a mile, however, the groom still failed to appear, Diana felt a twinge of concern. Could Devil have thrown him? As skilled as James seemed to be, Devil was a brute and was known to throw any rider he could.

Diana pulled Lucky Lady to a halt and turned to look over her shoulder the way she had come. Nothing. She caught her lower lip between her teeth, hesitating between the desire to be on her own, as always, and a sense of responsibility. Perhaps she should ride back and make certain the poor man was all right.

Then, as Diana was about to turn Lucky Lady around, she heard a horse neigh just over the ridge. Her eyes narrowed. That sounded suspiciously like Devil. But how could he be ahead of her? Perhaps it was someone else trespassing on her father's land. Diana urged her mount forward. She would see who was over the next ridge, and then she would go back and look for James.

As Lady Diana topped the ridge, she suddenly jerked on the reins, causing Lucky Lady to whinny in protest. Diana scarcely noticed. Instead, she was roused to fury at the sight that greeted her eyes. The groom was sitting on Devil, waiting for her under an old chestnut tree. Her first impulse was to turn Lucky Lady and wheel away. But that smacked of cowardice, and Diana had never run from anything in her life. Except James. Well, she would not run again. Diana urged her mare forward, the glint of battle in her eyes.

"Hallo, James," Diana said curtly. "I thought you were supposed to be following me."

James lowered his eyes meekly, but Diana had the distinct impression he was laughing at her as he said, "Aye, miss, but you were so fast, you see, I feared I couldn't catch up with you. And they told me you always ride this way, so I took a shortcut o' sorts to get here beforehand like. So as not to keep you waiting."

"And what would you have done if I hadn't come riding this way?" Diana demanded.

"Why then I s'pose I'd have been out of a job," James answered meekly.

"Well, I almost didn't," Diana told him crossly. "When you didn't appear behind me, I thought something must have happened to you, and I almost rode back to see."

Now a strange gleam lit the groom's eyes, and he all but grinned as he said, "You'd have gone back for me? Why, m'lady, I'd no notion you'd grown so fond of me, already."

"I am not fond of you!" Diana shouted in exasperation.

"But you'd have gone back to look for me," James pointed out ingenuously.

He eased his horse closer to Diana's, and she felt herself grow unaccountably warm inside. Nervously, she tried to move away.

"I'd have gone back for any servant on this estate," Diana temporized. Then, because he was coming closer still, and she could feel her color rising, Diana added impatiently, "Come, we've wasted too much time already. I want to go for a run."

And with no look back at James, Diana set Lucky Lady to gallop again. James watched her for a moment, and then he chuckled just before he set Devil to follow.

Eventually, Diana's ire wore off, and she drew Lucky Lady to a halt, aware that she had ridden her mare harder and faster than usual. It scarcely surprised Diana to discover that James was not the least bit tired out and that Devil gleamed with sweat but showed every sign of being ready to go farther.

To Diana's surprise, James made no sly comment about the ride, but only looked around as though memorizing where they had ended up. To her even greater surprise, Diana heard herself offering the man an apology.

"I'm sorry to have brought you so far," Diana said. "The horses will have a long ride back."

James shrugged and looked up at the sky, narrowing his eyes at the bright sunlight. "It's a nice day," he said calmly. "Happen I'll enjoy the break from mucking out the stables."

Now Diana looked at him, really looked at him. There was no playfulness, but no arrogance either in her gaze as she studied James. By not so much as a flicker of his eyelids did James betray any discomfort at her scrutiny. If anything, he seemed amused. But then, he didn't have anything to be uncomfortable about, Diana thought. His hair was dark and glossy, and seemed almost to curl at the ends. His eyes were deep, dark, and far seeing—the sort of eyes a girl could get lost in, if he weren't just a groom. The face was a strong one, and the habit of meekness did not sit easily, Diana thought. Nor did his broad shoulders want to round in deference, or the strong hands betray anything except an expectation of obedience from Devil. His hips . . .

But there Diana broke off her scrutiny, her color rising as she realized just what it was she was doing. This was absurd. He was merely a servant. And yet, he held her attention in a way that the young men of her own set never had. If only . . .

"I'm no more'nt a man." James broke into her thoughts with a lazy, amused smile.

Diana looked at him, fury in her eyes, now that he had dared notice, dared put into words what she had been doing. "It is quite clear to me you are nothing more nor less than a man," she said, her voice cold as ice.

James pretended to shiver. "Yes'm," he said. Then, with all apparent meekness, he added, "I was just going to say that I was merely a man, though I guess what with only knowing the gentry, you haven't seen very many of those. Mostly flowers you've seen, tulips and such."

Diana choked back a burst of laughter. She would not encourage his impertinence, she would not! And yet Diana could not help thinking of the young men of the neighborhood who vied with one another to wear the most absurd fashions from London and pay her the most absurd compliments.

Now James moved his horse closer. "I'm thinking not many of them tulips have ever thought to do this," he said.

Diana had time to move, she really did. And she could have used her crop to push him away. Instead, Diana sat very still on her horse and waited. She was not in the least surprised when his free arm went around her and his lips closed over hers. This time his kiss was gentle, seductive, teasing. He nibbled at her lower lip, his tongue dancing over the corners of her mouth. And when her lips parted, his tongue darted inside, unable to resist the invitation.

When James lifted his head, Diana stared up at him, bewildered. Her chest heaved as she tried to draw a breath. "How dare you?" she asked. "How dare you mock me like that?"

But his eyes weren't mocking her. Instead, they held bewilderment as great as her own—and something more, something that frightened Diana because it wasn't the bold brashness she expected. It was almost as though James looked strangely humbled. And when he reached for her again, she didn't draw back.

This time the kiss was deeper and stirred emotions and physical sensations Diana had never known before. When James drew back first this time, he said, looking down into her passion-glazed eyes, "You'll not be what your husband was expecting, I'll be bound."

That broke the spell, and now Diana pushed James away as hard as she could. Shame caused her face to color a deep red, and she wheeled Lucky Lady round as quickly as she could. Then she pressed the hapless mare into galloping toward home and the safety of the stable yard.

But no place would ever be safe again, and Diana knew it. Behind her she could hear James calling to her to be careful, but she ignored him. Careful? Dear God, the man had ravished her senses and caused her to come close to losing her mind! How could he tell her to be careful?

Had she not been so preoccupied, Diana would have seen the hazard and would have known to go around it. But she did not. Too late, Diana realized that Lucky Lady had bunched herself to jump, and it was only when they rose into the air that Diana saw the child on the other side of the fence.

Chapter Four

❧

Diana tried to guide Lucky Lady safely past the child, but she had begun the maneuver too late. A sickening crunch told her that Lucky Lady's hooves had connected with the boy's skull.

In moments, Diana was off Lucky Lady's back, the horse tethered to the fence, and she on her knees beside him. A nearby curse told her that James had done the same. Quickly, his hands moved over the boy, feeling his brow, checking for signs of life.

"Will he live?" Diana asked James, her face white with shock.

She felt rather than saw the curt nod he gave. There was a slight hesitation, and then the groom added, "Happen I think he will. Do you know who he is? Where he lives?"

Diana nodded. "One of our tenants. The cottage is just down the hill."

James scooped the boy up into his arms. He was young, scarcely ten, the groom thought. "Bring the horses," he said curtly, then started down the road without looking back to see if Diana would obey his sharply uttered command.

For a moment Diana stared after him, her mouth open. The she hastened to grab the reins of both horses. She had to catch up with James, show him which cottage to go to, explain to the family that what had happened to the child was her fault, not his.

James did not acknowledge her presence with anything more than a nod. His own face showed the same signs of strain as hers. Only when the child in his arms began to stir did some of the grim lines about his mouth begin to disappear, and Diana realized he had been finding it as difficult to breathe as she did.

"Mama," the boy whimpered in James's arms.

To Diana's surprise, the groom's voice was soft and gentle as James replied, "Hush, my lad, hush. You'll see your mama soon, I promise you. A minute or two more and we'll be at your door."

And they were, for James was walking as fast as he could, not caring whether Diana had to run to keep up with him. All his attention seemed to be bent on the child in his arms, and Diana found herself unaccountably touched by that.

Suddenly, she realized James was speaking to her again. "You'd best tether the horses and knock on the door," he said curtly.

But the door was already being opened and a woman hurrying out to them. "My baby!" she cried. "Whatever's happened to my baby?"

Diana shot an agonized look at James, who was striding past the woman toward the door of the cottage. "An accident," he told her in the same soft voice he had used with the boy. "The horse took the fence and clipped him. But he's coming round, and I think he'll be fine."

"No thanks to you!" the woman cried as she followed and bent over her son where James had placed him on the one bed in the room. "You oughtn't to have taken that fence if my Peter was there!"

"I didn't see him," James replied humbly.

Abruptly, Diana closed her mouth, which had been gaping open in astonishment. She stepped forward, a gleam of determination in her eye. "It wasn't—" she began, but James cut her short.

"It weren't intentional," James said, smoothly cutting across Diana's words to prevent her confession. "I'd give anything to have it undone."

The woman's voice softened. "Aye, well, I suppose it weren't your fault. Peter's always underfoot, and well I know it. Probably went over to the fence to get a better look at milady as she went riding by. Horse mad, he is. His papa says maybe he'll grow up to be one of the grooms up to the grand house when he's older."

"And I will, too," the boys high-pitched voice broke in, startling all of them.

Diana fought an urge to crowd close to the boy. Instead, she stood back to let his mother do so. She bit the inside of her mouth to keep from crying out, so great was her distress. And when James put his hand over hers in comfort, Diana did not pull it away. Nor did she resist when he stroked her cheek with the other hand and said, "He'll be all right, I'm sure he will."

Diana nodded, unable to speak. Only when the boy's mother turned to her, a tremulous smile on her lips and unshed tears gleaming in her eyes, could Diana find her voice. "The doctor," she said. "We should go and get the doctor to come look at him."

"Aye, that would be a good notion," James seconded her. "I'll go, if you like."

"Do you know where he lives?" Diana asked doubtfully.

"No," James admitted.

"Then I'll go," Diana told him briskly. "You stay and see if you can help here."

Then, before he could protest, Diana was gone from the cottage. James followed her outside, but only to be certain she was steady on her horse. He let her ride away. This was something he knew she needed to do. James went back into the cottage and set about making peace with the boy's mother.

Later, when the doctor had been to the cottage and pronounced Peter to have a hard head and to be on his way to recovery, James had paid the man because Diana realized to her mortification that she had no coins on her. He also gave a few to the boy's mother. "Just in case he needs anything while he mends," he told her gently.

Outside, James helped Diana mount Lucky Lady, and this time she let him, without protest. As they both edged their horses in the direction of the Manor, however, Diana decided to ask him the questions that had been bothering her since he first carried the boy into the cottage.

"Why did you take the blame for me?" she asked.

He shrugged. "Happen my shoulders are broader than yours," he said with a grimace.

Diana reached out and put a hand on his arm. "No, really," she said. "Tell me why. I've the feeling, at times, that you don't even like me."

James looked at her then, and his clear brown eyes held much more than Diana could read. Or perhaps they held more than she wanted to read. At last he said, goaded, "Perhaps I felt it was my fault. If I hadn't kissed you, you wouldn't have let your horse run away like that. You'd have seen the boy beforehand."

They stared at one another. Then, as though embarrassed

by his outburst, James shrugged again and said softly, "I don't dislike you, m'lady. But I'm only a groom, m'lady, and shouldn't ought to forget my place."

That set her at a distance. In a few well-chosen words James had reminded Diana of the vast gulf between them. He was a groom, and she was a lady, the daughter of an earl, betrothed to a duke. Suddenly, Diana frowned. "How did you come to have so many coins on you?" she demanded. "Rawlins can't have even paid you yet for any of the work you've done here."

Now James refused to meet her eyes. "I didn't come penniless, m'lady," he protested. "I'm not the sort to leave my last post without funds to support myself until I found another."

"Yes, James, your last post," Diana said with narrowed eyes. "Tell me about your last post."

It was James's turn to color up, and he tugged at the collar of his shirt as if it had suddenly grown too tight. "My last post?" he echoed as though trying to buy himself time.

"Yes, your last post," Diana replied sweetly. "Was it a good one? Did they pay well? Were you a groom, and did you have to muck out the stables?"

James looked away, and Diana had the distinct impression that he would have liked to strangle her. "It ain't none of your affair, my lady," he said stiffly.

She ought to have let matters alone. Some inner demon, however, prompted Diana to ask, "Failed to give satisfaction, did you?"

Now an odd gleam lit the groom's eyes, and a slow smile spread across his face as he said, "So far as I know, my lady, I have never failed to give satisfaction in my life."

Diana colored up to the roots of her hair. Good Lord, the man made his answer sound impossibly intimate! She could not meet his eyes and tried to look everywhere but at his face. Suddenly, Diana could not bear the warmth that seemed almost to radiate from James, and she set Lucky Lady to gallop toward home.

James chuckled softly and then set Devil in pursuit. An observer might have been pardoned for believing James was pleased by what had just occurred.

Diana reached the stable yard first, but only by a short margin. James was close upon her heels and off Devil by the time she had dismounted. It was only when she refused his offer of help with Lucky Lady that Diana realized her father was standing nearby, watching herself and James.

"Papa!" she exclaimed. "What are you doing here?"

"Your mother sent me out to discover where you were. It is past time for you to be in the house and changed," the Earl of Westcott replied dryly. "Your sisters are already in the parlor, receiving visitors."

"Who?" Diana demanded warily.

"Mrs. Fairwood and her daughter," the earl replied with an understanding smile. "No one you need fear," he added, referring to one of the more persistent young men in the neighborhood, who had fixed his interest on Diana in spite of her betrothal.

"I shall go in straightaway," Diana said and moved to go past her father.

The Earl of Westcott let her go, and then he turned his attention to James. "You're the new groom, aren't you?" he asked, staring closely at James.

James nodded, keeping his face toward the horses as he removed their saddles. "Aye," he said.

"And your last post was with the Duke of Berenford?" Westcott persisted.

Again James nodded. The Earl of Westcott's next words

struck him with the force of a blow. "You have the look of the family about you."

James struggled to find his voice. "Do I?" he asked unsteadily.

Westcott chuckled. "One of old Berenford's by-blows, I collect. And the new duke meaning to do well by you. No need to color up, my boy. I've no quarrel with that. Explained in his letter, he did, that he'd like his future wife, my daughter Diana, to become accustomed to you before the two are married. Wants her to have a servant she knows about the place. Knacky notion, that. Plus, I've no doubt he hopes you'll tell him a bit or two about my girl. Tell me, my boy, how do you find my daughter?"

If James had appeared uncomfortable before, now he seemed positively speechless. The Earl of Westcott waited patiently for his answer, and finally James found his voice. It sounded almost strangled, however, as he replied, "Lady Diana is an extraordinary young lady. Very beautiful, my lord."

"And rather hot to hand?" Westcott added dryly.

James tugged at the collar of his shirt. "A mite," he agreed. "High-spirited, I'd say."

The Earl of Westcott pursed his lips judiciously a moment before he said with deceptive innocence, "And do you think those qualities will appeal to His Grace, the duke?"

James stared at the earl blankly. He seemed stunned by the question. An instant later, his shoulders were hunched, and he turned back to the horses as he answered over his shoulder, "How should I know m'lord? I can't read His Grace's mind, now can I?"

"Yes, but if you've been with him for some time, as he said, I should think you would know something of the man.

His character, that sort of thing," Westcott persisted in the same mild tone as before.

It was perhaps fortunate that James was not looking at the earl. The twinkle in his lordship's eyes would have unnerved the poor groom more than ever. As it was, James's voice was a trifle unsteady, almost defiant as he said, "I s'pose I'd have to say that His Grace will like her ladyship very well. Very well, indeed. Now, t'other way round, I'm not so certain," he added in warning.

"Ah, but I am," the Earl of Westcott said, mischief apparent in his voice. "I think my Diana will like him very well, indeed. After her initial shock upon meeting him, that is."

That startled James into looking at the earl. What he saw there did not reassure him. Not even when Westcott added smoothly, "I was just thinking that Diana may notice the family resemblance, that's all. But don't worry, Diana's broad-minded enough to be able to accept one of Berenford's old by-blows as her groom. I just hope there's enough difference between the two of you, in appearance, of course, that she doesn't confuse you, one for the other."

With that the Earl of Westcott turned on his heel and walked back toward the house, whistling cheerfully, as James stared after him in stunned amazement.

"Close your mouth or you'll catch you some flies in there," Rawlins advised, coming over to James. "I won't ask what his lordship said to you, but he seems in a powerful pleased mood. Keep it up and you'll go far. Now hurry and put the horses in, then finish mucking out the stable."

"Yes, Mr. Rawlins," James said hastily, and hurried to do as he was bid.

Chapter Five

No one was prepared for the arrival of Miss Tibbles, not even Lady Westcott. At precisely 9:48 the next morning, someone demanded admittance to Westcott Manor, and the door was opened by an astonished footman.

"The family is not yet at home," he stammered haplessly. "If you would care to leave your card or call later . . ."

His voice trailed off as his superior appeared. Mr. Crandall took one look at the woman who stood on the doorstep. He had been with the family a long time and recognized at once the class of person before him. Mr. Crandall's face took on a pained expression. He turned to the footman. "You may go," he said. Then he addressed the woman. "I collect you are the new governess. Miss Tibbles, I believe?"

The woman gave Mr. Crandall, as he later described it to the housekeeper, the most mortifying inspection he had ever endured. Then she nodded briskly and said, "You'll do. You may announce me to Lady Westcott. I shall wait here while you do so. You may also have a footman bring my trunks into the hall."

Mr. Crandall was not by nature a timid man. Had he been, he should never have been entrusted with the post he now held. But he was a shrewd man, and he knew he had met his match. He contented himself with lifting one eyebrow disdainfully, sniffing ever so slightly, and turning on his heel without another word. Behind him, he was certain he could feel Miss Tibble's eyes boring into his back, a satisfied smile upon her face.

Still, there was one consolation, Mr. Crandall told himself as he went upstairs to convey the information to Lady Westcott that the new governess had arrived. Miss Tibbles looked to be the first governess who could possibly tame the Westcott girls. In his opinion it was a pity she hadn't arrived a few years earlier.

Upstairs, Lady Westcott received the news of Miss Tibbles's arrival with a shriek of dismay. Still, her maid helped her dress with surprising speed, and there was not a hair out of place when Lady Westcott reached the foyer to greet the new governess.

"Miss Tibbles, I presume?" Lady Westcott said, looking the woman up and down.

The woman inclined her head. "Lady Westcott, I presume?" she said in reply.

Lady Westcott smiled thinly. The battle lines were drawn. She would not be overset in her own house and certainly not by a mere governess. "You are surprisingly early," she said. "We did not expect you until much later in the day."

"I hope this is not a late-rising household," Miss Tibbles countered. "I cannot abide a lazy household."

Lady Westcott bristled. "We rise early here," she said sharply, "but that does not mean we are in the habit of welcoming visitors before noon. Not," she added with narrowed eyes, "that you are a visitor. My sister spoke highly of your qualifications as a governess."

"And Lady Brisbane spoke at great length of the high spirits of your daughters," Miss Tibbles replied with equally narrowed eyes. "I always begin as I mean to go on, and I have found it wise to arrive before the girls in question expect me. That is why I took the stage a day early. Having arrived in the village late last night, however, I considered it more prudent to spend the night at the inn, there, rather than arrive at an hour that must be disagreeable to you and which would give the girls the night to make their plans for my welcome."

For a moment Lady Westcott considered the possibility that she had made a great error in hiring Miss Tibbles to teach Barbara, Penelope, and Rebecca. Still, the woman was here, and she seemed quite formidable.

"I shall send for my daughters," Lady Westcott said, "and tell them you are here. No doubt you will wish to be taken up to your room to freshen up before you meet them."

"I am fully prepared to meet them now," Miss Tibbles said with a smile that did not bode well for the girls. "If you will direct me to the nursery, I shall go and find them myself."

With a sinking sensation Lady Westcott turned and led the way up the stairs. On the stairs Lady Westcott tried once again to assert her control of the situation. "I collect you have a great deal of experience dealing with young ladies?" Lady Westcott said, the hint of a question in her voice.

Miss Tibbles sniffed. "A great deal. It seems I am generally called in when the young ladies in question have gotten completely out of hand. Then, the moment I've gotten them under control again, I'm told my services are no longer necessary. It seems that while everyone wants well-behaved daughters, far too many parents are so mistakenly tenderhearted as to oppose my methods. There is no gratitude left in this world, Lady Westcott. I do hope you are not going to prove as difficult as some of my previous employers."

The sinking sensation grew. Suddenly, Lady Westcott began to think it would be an excellent notion to move forward her trip to London with Diana. What, after all, was there to keep her here, now that Miss Tibbles had arrived?

The possibility that she did not wish to be present during the clash of wills between Miss Tibbles and her daughters, a clash that would surely occur, was something Lady Westcott refused to admit, even to herself. Instead, she told herself that a little extra time in London, to give Diana a bit more town polish, would be an excellent notion. She also managed to persuade herself that Lord Westcott would be pleased. Lady Westcott had a great talent for self-deception.

Upstairs, the girls heard the commotion below, and one of the maids, who was their friend, ran upstairs with the news of Miss Tibbles's arrival. With scarcely a word spoken between them, the girls arranged themselves in the tableau they wished to present to their new governess.

Diana sat on the window seat, staring out at the grounds of Westcott Manor. Annabelle perused the latest issue of Ackermann's Repository, a hint of worry in her furrowed brow. Her younger sisters dearly hoped her rigid sense of duty would not cause her to thrust a spoke into their plans.

Barbara sat at the nursery table with the twins, a history book in hand. Rebecca and Penelope sat demurely opposite one another, as they copied out a mathematics problem from the text their last governess had tried to impose upon them. That was how Lady Westcott and Miss Tibbles found them.

"Oh, dear," Lady Westcott murmured under her breath, recognizing only too well the signs of mischief afoot.

Miss Tibbles stepped into the room and looked around. Her eyes narrowed as she took in the pleasant tableau, and she nodded twice, as though in silent satisfaction.

"Well, you've some small degree of intelligence, at any rate," she said to the girls They exchanged demure smiles, and Miss Tibbles's lips thinned into a smile of her own as she added sharply, "Most of my charges haven't the sense to pretend they'll cooperate with me or that they've any interest in learning. I've no doubt you girls possess active imaginations as well. So I give you fair warning now that any surprises in my bed will result in a bucket of cold water being dumped on each of you as you sleep."

Rebecca and Penelope looked at one another with wide, wary eyes. Barbara stiffened, and Miss Tibbles made a mental note to be particularly wary of that one. Diana pretended to ignore the entire conversation.

It was left to Annabelle to reply. She cast a minatory eye on the twins, then said softly, "I am certain, Miss Tibbles, that my sisters will give you no cause for such treatment of them."

Miss Tibbles sniffed. "That's as may be. But I like to begin as I mean to go on, and I find that giving such a warning at the start often avoids a great deal of trouble later on. Now, I dislike to be rude, but, Lady Westcott, I should like you to leave so that I can begin my lessons with your daughters." She paused and considered Diana and Annabelle a moment before she added, "I've no doubt that your eldest two girls could benefit from further study as well. They are quite welcome to remain."

That did it. Diana scrambled with unseemly haste from her perch on the window seat and headed for the door. "I'm due to go out riding," she said, ignoring the angry, imploring looks from her younger sisters.

Annabelle was more dignified but she, too, rose to her feet and started for the door. "And I, I need to help Mama in the stillroom," she said, blushing, with a fine disregard for the truth.

Miss Tibbles watched them go with a satisfied smile. Then, having successfully routed the elder girls, she turned toward her charges, and once again her eyes narrowed as she advanced toward the table to begin the task of whipping the girls into shape.

Halfway down the stairs, well out of earshot of the nursery, Diana turned to Lady Westcott and said, "Oh, Mama! How could you employ someone like Miss Tibbles?"

Lady Westcott sniffed and replied, defensively, "Miss Tibbles comes highly recommended, and I happen to think, as does my sister, Ariana, that Miss Tibbles will be just the one to help your sisters become proper young ladies."

Diana and Annabelle exchanged glances. "Yes, but Mama," Annabelle ventured to protest, "don't you think her a . . . a trifle heavy to hand?"

Lady Westcott glared at her second eldest daughter. "I think," she said severely, managing to forget her own earlier qualms on the subject, "that a heavy hand is precisely what is required to bring your sisters to heel. They have run wild far too long, and it is time they learned to be ladies."

"But Papa—" Diana began.

Lady Westcott cut her short. "I am certain," Lady Westcott said virtuously, "that your father will be most pleased when he meets Miss Tibbles and has the opportunity to see her virtues. And don't roll your eyes at me, Diana. He will be pleased."

Lady Westcott might have been right, had Miss Tibbles

not mistaken Lord Westcott for one of the servants when she descended to the ground floor shortly before lunchtime. As it was, she was almost dismissed before the girls had a chance to play even one trick upon her.

"Delwinia," Lord Westcott said warningly.

"Oh, dear, Miss Tibbles, this is my husband, Lord West-cott. Adam, this is Miss Tibbles, the new governess," Lady Westcott said hastily.

"Ain't half-witted, is she?" Westcott demanded, gazing sharply at the woman before him.

Miss Tibbles drew in her breath with a hiss. "It was a perfectly natural mistake, I assure you. Anyone might have mistaken you for the gardener, dressed as you are. As for me, I shall have you know I come highly recommended. Highly recommended," she snapped out in reply. "I had my choice of positions, and if it were not for dear Lady Bris-bane's belief that my services are needed here, which I have seen for myself with my own eyes, I should leave im-mediately."

"Lady Brisbane!" Westcott said with a snort as he turned to his wife. "I should have known your sister would be meddling again!"

"Dear, she only wished to help, and you must admit that we do need help," Lady Westcott temporized. "We've yet to keep a governess above six months."

"Well, I shall stay longer than that, I can promise you," Miss Tibbles said with a determined gleam in her eyes.

Lord and Lady Westcott looked at one another with a sinking sensation, so that they did not see Annabelle and Diana exchange curt nods that would have otherwise sig-naled to them the impending disaster.

"Don't you have something to do?" Lord Westcott asked

her. "See to the girls or something? You surely cannot be finished with your duties for the day."

Miss Tibbles lifted one finely arched eyebrow and regarded the Earl of Westcott with a look that had been known to reduce the most reprobate girl to demure obedience. "I *am* pursuing my duties," she said haughtily. "I came to request that certain supplies be purchased so that I can properly instruct your daughters in the skills they will need as adults. I have prepared a list."

It was only then that Lord and Lady Westcott noticed the piece of paper Miss Tibbles had been holding in her hands. Diana and Annabelle wisely chose this moment to withdraw to a small parlor out of sight and hearing of the three adults to consult as to the proper course of action regarding Miss Tibbles.

"We cannot leave the younger girls to her mercy," Annabelle said, wringing her hands together.

"No, nor Miss Tibbles to theirs," Diana retorted bluntly. "Which means we must do something."

"But what?" Annabelle asked anxiously. "I cannot see that any prank will drive that woman off. Indeed, it is far more likely to persuade her that her services are more necessary than ever." Annabelle paused, then suggested hesitantly, "Perhaps we could persuade Barbara and the twins to pretend she has already succeeded and that she is no longer needed?"

The two girls looked at one another and at the same moment sighed and shook their heads. "You know it could never work," Diana said. "The twins might be able to carry off such a sham, but Barbara would be certain to give away the game. Particularly as Miss Tibbles seems too shrewd to believe them easily." It was Diana's turn to pause and con sider the matter, then say, "We must persuade Miss Tibbles that she does not wish to succeed."

"Yes, but how can we possibly do that, Diana?" Annabelle asked doubtfully, mistrusting the look in her older sister's eyes.

Diana's next words fully justified that distrust. "We must simply make Miss Tibbles think that madness runs through the family," Diana replied with wide-eyed innocence. "Surely, even she would be daunted by that prospect."

"I don't think Mama would like that," Annabelle said. "And what if you succeed and Miss Tibbles carries the tale back to London with her? How will the girls ever get husbands then?"

"Oh, pooh!" Diana said with a shrug. "It only wants a little resolution. Mama will be just as relieved as we are to have Miss Tibbles gone. As for tales, why the moment they see the girls, people will know they are not mad. As for me and you, well, I am already betrothed, and you will be as soon as I am safely shackled to Berenford."

"Yes, but what if he hears the rumors and cries off?" Annabelle asked.

"Who? Do you mean Winsborough?" Diana asked teasingly.

"No, Berenford! As you very well know," Annabelle retorted impatiently. "What if he should cry off?"

Diana turned her back on her sister and shrugged again. "He will not," she said in a small voice. "And if he were so foolish, I should not care."

"Yes, but I would," Annabelle replied with some exasperation. "I want to marry Lord Winsborough, and you know very well that Mama and Papa will not let me do so until you are safely wed."

Diana turned to face her sister and grinned. "I promise,"

she said, "this shall not cause Berenford to cry off. I just wish to free the girls from Miss Tibbles. And you must help me. Here is what we must do . . . ."

Chapter Six

~

James had no warning. One moment Lady Diana was mounted on her horse, waiting for him to spring into the saddle, and the next moment she was heading for the main house. Worse, far worse, she did not halt at the front steps, but mounted them on her horse without the slightest hesitation. The front door had been left ajar, and Lady Diana went easily inside. Hastily, James dismounted Devil and ran up the steps to follow his apparently demented charge.

In the foyer Diana hid a smile of satisfaction. Annabelle, however reluctantly, had done her part. She had managed to get Miss Tibbles downstairs and into the small parlor off the entryway. As planned, both Annabelle and Miss Tibbles appeared instantly to discover the source of the strange sounds they could not help but hear.

At the top of the stairs Barbara stood ready to play her part. Diana only hoped that Annabelle had coached her properly, and that Barbara did not think to embellish her role to the point of straining credulity.

But Barbara was restrained. "Oh, dear, Diana. Not again!" she sighed.

Diana merely stared at the wall ahead of her blankly. Miss Tibbles regarded each of the three girls in turn, and then settled on Annabelle as the one most likely to give her an intelligible answer. "What, may I ask, is going on here?" she demanded severely.

Annabelle appeared to hesitate. She seemed to cast agonized looks at first Diana and then Barbara. Finally, in a voice that caught, she said, "We had hoped no one would know. We had hoped Diana had outgrown these episodes. It's been more than a year, after all. It's not like any of us has these episodes often. I only walk in my sleep. And Barbara, well, if she occasionally gives vent to odd speech, we just ignore it. And the twins, well, I'm sure that by the time they make their come-out, we will have found some solution."

Miss Tibbles stared at Annabelle piercingly, but the girl kept her eyes on the ground. Miss Tibbles then circled Diana, as if staring at her from another angle might give her a clue as to what was going on. Finally, she turned to James and said, "Who are you?"

In the act of reaching for Lucky Lady's bridle, James turned a helpless gaze on Miss Tibbles, only to be met with scathing, disparaging scrutiny. Instantly, his back was up. How dare she look at him as if he were dirt? Just as suddenly, James felt a sinking sensation in the pit of his stomach. He knew this woman—knew this woman only too well. And unfortunately, she knew him.

Hastily, James bent his head down and averted his eyes. "Me? I'm the groom what's supposed to ride wif Lady Diana," he said gruffly.

"Are you now? What an interesting occupation for a man such as yourself," Miss Tibbles replied.

Her tone of voice was such that James could not help but look at her. A knowing gleam sparkled in her eyes as they narrowed to study him. Hastily, he looked away again. Had she recognized him? What would she say?

But Miss Tibbles said nothing. She merely turned to Diana and said with force, "Your horse belongs outside. As does your groom. Leave the house at once!"

Diana looked at her with limpid eyes. "But Lucky Lady wants to be in here," she said. "We have both come in for tea."

Now Barbara came halfway down the stairs to say, "It's best to humor her, Miss Tibbles. We always do."

Miss Tibbles looked at Barbara and replied dryly, "I daresay you do." Then she turned to Diana again and said sharply, "I shall count to five, Lady Diana. If, by then, you have not exited this house by the front door, I shall slap your horse as hard as I can in the hopes that he will throw you and knock some sense into that head of yours!"

Startled, Diana was betrayed into looking at Miss Tibbles. The woman began to count and lift her hand. Diana had no doubt she meant precisely what she said. Hastily, Diana turned Lucky Lady and fled the house. If Miss Tibbles slapped Lucky Lady, there was no knowing what the mare might do, and if he did throw her, Papa would be certain to get rid of the mare. And that was a thought Diana could not bear.

James hurried to follow, careful to keep his face averted from Miss Tibbles as he went. Outside, he hastily mounted Devil as Diana set her horse to a gallop and raced across the lawn. Thank God, James thought, that he had a good notion where she meant to go. Being a groom was proving far more difficult a task than he had ever imagined it could be.

Eventually, Diana came to a halt near the stream. She was surprisingly relieved to discover James so close behind her. For once she did not protest when he helped her down from her horse, or object when he took the reins to tether Lucky Lady as well as his own mount to a nearby tree. James was angry, and rightfully so, she thought.

"What on earth could have possessed you to do such a damn fool thing?" James demanded in exasperation.

Diana started as though stung. "I had a very good reason," she countered.

James crossed his arms over his chest. "What reason?" he demanded. "Were you trying to see if you could lame Lucky Lady by taking her onto polished marble floors? Or perhaps you were trying to show me, and everyone else, that you are wanting in wits?"

To his surprise Diana flushed and half turned away. "Precisely," she said over her shoulder.

That brought James straight up. "Precisely?" he echoed incredulously. "Why? Why the devil would you want anyone to think you mad?"

Diana could not look at him. "I . . . I thought perhaps it would discourage the new governess."

"Miss Tibbles?" James asked in disbelief.

Now Diana turned to look at him, her eyes narrowed in suspicion. "How did you know her name?"

Instantly, James realized his error. "I . . . I, the servants talk, of course," he said hastily. "All of us have heard her name."

"Even out in the stables?" Diana asked with a frown.

"Of course," James repeated, wishing it were true. Had he known the name of the woman who had appeared at the house that morning, nothing could have made him cross the threshold. He dare not admit, however, that there was any other way he could have known her name. Instead, James pressed an attack.

"Why would you want to drive away your sisters' new

governess?" he asked. "I've heard tell they're badly in need of one."

"You know nothing of the matter," Diana retorted, her chin lifted defiantly.

Abruptly, James's voice changed. With unexpected gentleness he said, "Tell me, then."

Diana hesitated, but the need to explain was strong. "I suppose you will think it silly," she said, "but my sisters are dear to me, and I should not like to see their spirits broken by Miss Tibbles."

"If they've even half your strength, I cannot think that will happen," James replied with the same gentleness as before.

Now Diana looked at James, really looked at him, and found herself thinking what a strange groom he was. He was far too handsome to be a groom. And too gentle, Diana thought. Though perhaps that was a useful feature with horses, she conceded. But it was more than that. It was the way he spoke, the words he used, that made Diana think James unusual.

As she stared at James, he reached out for her, and it suddenly seemed the most natural thing in the world to Diana to walk into his arms and be held against his strong chest. The arms that closed around her did not hesitate, but rather reassured her with their certainty. Were anyone to see them, it would be a scandal, but Diana didn't care. Right now she needed comfort, and James could give it.

As for James, a series of mixed emotions crossed his face. Delight at Diana's trust, worry that matters were getting out of hand, desire to do more than just hold her pressed against his chest. Slowly, gently, giving her time to refuse, James bent his head downward and kissed Diana's forehead, then the tip of her nose, and finally he captured her lips with his own. A groan escaped the groom at the sweetness he found there.

To the devil, he thought, with propriety and all other such considerations! James dipped deeper, seducing Diana with the fervency of his kiss. She did not resist. How could she? Not when the merest touch of his lips made her want more. Not when his arms tightened and she found herself pressed invitingly against every lean muscle of his body. Not when the loneliness in her soul cried out to join the loneliness she sensed in his.

It didn't matter that James was a mere groom. It didn't matter that Diana was to be married in less than two months. What mattered was that for the first time in her life Diana felt as though she could be whole. As though she were accepted and wanted and cared for just for herself, not for the person someone else wanted her to be. And because she must soon marry and be what someone else, her new husband, wanted her to be, this gift was all the more precious to Diana.

Now it was Diana's arms that stole around James and held him close against the curves of her body. It was Diana who kissed James with all the fervor she possessed. And it was James who finally called a halt to their madness, though only after his hand had wandered to cup the soft ripeness of her breasts. Then, with a fierce groan, he broke free and set Diana away from him.

"We cannot," he said softly, breathing hard.

"Why not?" Diana pleaded. "Who need know?"

James shook his head and took another step away from her. "You don't even know what you're asking, m'lady. Or who you're asking it of. We cannot do this. You'd be sorry before we even reached your home. And I'd be turned away, rightly so, without a second thought."

Diana averted her face, mortified. "I hadn't thought," she said. "You'd be the one to bear the blame, even if it were all my fault. I'm sorry, James. I'd no right to ask such a thing of you."

James wanted to step forward and take Diana in his arms again. He wanted to kiss away the pain in her voice and the loneliness that echoed his own. But he couldn't. Not here, not now, not this way. Instead, he made his voice emotionless as he said with the proper deference of a groom, "Time we were headed back to the house, m'lady. They'll be worried about you by now."

Diana looked at James and nodded. She was so grateful that he did not smirk or leer or look at her in anger. So she swallowed the other words that came to mind, words he would only reject or that might embarrass him, and nodded.

"I suppose I'd best go home and accept my scoldings before my parents grow even more upset," Diana said quietly. "But before we do, I'd like to stop and see if that boy, Peter, is all right."

James smiled at her, and Diana felt her heart inexplicably soar. "I'd like to know that myself," he said.

Meekly, James helped his mistress mount. Was it only her imagination, Diana wondered, that his hands seemed to linger on her foot as he settled her on her horse?

Later, after they had visited Peter and assured themselves that he would be all right, James and Diana rode back to the stables. Diana hurried up to the house and crossed the threshold on tiptoe, in hopes of making it to her room unseen. Mama, however, was waiting for her.

"You will come into your father's library now," Lady Westcott said as the footman took her daughter's gloves and riding crop.

Diana meekly followed. Once inside the dark paneled

room, with the door securely shut, both the Earl and Countess of Westcott stared accusingly at their daughter.

"What the devil possessed you to take such a risk with Lucky Lady?" Westcott demanded. "She could have slipped on the polished marble and broken a leg!"

The countess regarded her husband with some exasperation, then said to Diana, "The more important question is why you should wish to have our new governess believe you mad. Fortunately," she added with malicious satisfaction, "Miss Tibbles has had sufficient experience with girls of your sort to know you were only pulling a prank on her."

"Does she blame Annabelle or Barbara?" Diana asked.

Lady Westcott smiled thinly. "No, her precise words were that she knew you had invented the notion and merely persuaded your sisters to follow."

A sense of relief passed through Diana. She straightened her shoulders and said, "I suppose it wasn't wise of me. I'm sorry. Shall I go and apologize?"

"Yes," Lady Westcott said, "you will do so directly you leave this room."

Diana turned to go, but her father's voice halted her. "Wait, my girl, we're not quite done," he said gruffly. "Your mother has news for you."

Diana looked at the countess, a question in her eyes. Lady Westcott hesitated, then plunged into the heart of the matter. "I have decided, that is your father and I have decided, that it would be best if we left for London as soon as possible. The day after tomorrow, in fact."

"What?" Diana stared at her mother in shock. "You are joking. Why must we go now? My wedding is not for a few weeks."

Lady Westcott sighed. "Surely you must realize, Diana, that there are any number of things to do before your wedding. You know very well that you need new clothes, and they must be fashionable ones. I cannot think what Berenford would say were he to see how you are dressed today."

Since Diana had never cared what she wore, she knew her mother's words were justified. And yet they simply served to set up her back.

Diana looked at her mother and said, "I won't go." Both Lord and Lady Westcott stared at their daughter, and she repeated her words. "I won't go. I want every moment of possible freedom before it comes to an end with my marriage to Berenford."

Now the Earl of Westcott came to his feet. There were many who mistook his habitually genial expression to mean that he had no force of will. No one seeing him now, however, could possibly make such a mistake. His voice was even and icy as he said, biting off his words precisely, "Diana, you will go to London with your mother, and you will go whenever she tells you to go. I will not have you shame our family by arriving at the altar with scarcely a decent rag to your back. You will go to the altar with all the dignity and pride that befits a daughter of the Earl of Westcott. Is that clear?"

Diana swallowed hard. "Yes, Papa," she said in a small voice.

"Good," Westcott said, the edge of steel still in his voice. "You will be ready to leave the day after tomorrow. The girls and I will follow with Miss Tibbles in a week or two, since Berenford prefers to be married in London."

Diana sighed. She knew, none better, how indulged she had been since the day of her birth. No other parents would have given her the same degree of freedom to run wild; few other parents would have shown the same degree of consideration in consulting her wishes concerning her marriage.

She was only too conscious that it was wrong of her to speak as she had now. Her parents wanted only the best for her. That didn't mean, however, that she had to like it.

Diana had just settled herself into this pose of meekness when her father spoiled it with his careless words. "One good thing about this, Diana," he said with a grin, "is that you needn't put up with that impertinent groom any longer."

And those simple words cast Diana's spirits down even further than she would have thought possible. Would he, she wondered, miss her?

Lady Westcott's voice broke into Diana's thoughts. "Now that we are finished here, Diana, you will go upstairs and apologize to Miss Tibbles."

"Yes, Mama."

But Miss Tibbles was nowhere to be found. She had set the twins and Barbara to doing sketches of one another and Annabelle, and then departed for, she said, a short walk. It seemed odd of Miss Tibbles to so shirk her responsibility, but Diana dutifully settled herself to wait.

Miss Tibbles, however, was not shirking her responsibility. She had known the moment she saw the so-called groom, James, that she must speak to him, and she did not believe in unnecessary delay. Therefore she set the girls to their work, then marched down to the stables the moment she saw Lady Diana return from her ride. In the stable yard Miss Tibbles informed Rawlins that he was to fetch James to speak with her at once.

"Yes'm," Rawlins said doubtfully. "He's a powerful lot of work to do."

"I shan't keep him long," Miss Tibbles said.

Rawlins nodded and went to fetch James. The moment the poor boy came out of the barn and saw Miss Tibbles, his color went pale, then red. He looked as though he wanted to turn tail and run, but instead swallowed hard and came to where Miss Tibbles stood waiting.

"Good. Now come along with me while I walk in the garden," Miss Tibbles said. "I can't think you want to talk here, where we might be overheard."

Miss Tibbles turned and headed toward the gardens, serene in the knowledge that James would follow. And he did, cap in hand, waiting for her to begin. When they were safely away from any interested ears, Miss Tibbles stopped and looked at James. After a thorough inspection that left him more abashed than ever, she said, "Now then, Jeremy Stowall, ninth Duke of Berenford, what the devil do you think you are about?"

Chapter Seven

~

"Well?" Miss Tibbles said impatiently. "I am waiting for an answer."

James, or rather the Duke of Berenford, sighed and ran a hand through his thick, dark hair. "I wanted to meet my bride," he said.

"There are more conventional ways of doing so," Miss Tibbles pointed out dryly.

Berenford stared down at the woman standing before him. "Yes, but then I shouldn't have gotten to know the real Lady Diana," he said. "I should only have gotten to know the one presented to the *ton*."

"Well, you can't go on at this much longer," Miss Tibbles said sternly. "What if you are found out? Just think how mortified the family would be, will be, when they realize the truth. And they will. What do you mean to do when you see Lady Diana in London?"

Berenford grinned, a twinkle in his dark eyes. "Perhaps she will think it a good joke. She does have a sense of humor, you know."

"Oh, yes, I know that very well," Miss Tibbles replied. "But you are a fool if you think it will be that easy to win her over after she discovers this May game you've been playing with her."

"We shall see," Berenford said confidently, thinking of the embrace he and Diana had shared by the stream.

"In any event," Miss Tibbles said, breaking into his thoughts, "I cannot permit this masquerade to continue. "I would be failing my duty to the family if I did not tell them who you are."

Now Berenford took her hand in his. "Please don't," he said. "I shall go away. The day after tomorrow. Just let the groom, James, take his leave of Lady Diana, first."

Miss Tibbles meant to refuse, she truly did. But even she was not impervious to Berenford's charm. "Do you care about the girl? At all?" she asked.

"I do," he answered sincerely. "More than I thought I could. I know you don't approve of my masquerade, Miss Tibbles, but I've seen a side of Diana I might otherwise never have known. And I think, yes, I truly think I am falling in love with her."

And then, because, despite her stern exterior, Miss Tibbles was really a romantic at heart, she patted his cheek and said with a sigh, "Very well. I give you until the day after tomorrow to take your leave. But if you are not gone by then, I shall tell the family precisely who you are!"

Berenford lifted Miss Tibbles off her feet and soundly bussed her on each cheek. Then, still grinning impudently, he set her back down and said, "You shan't regret it, Miss Tibbles."

"I'd better not," she replied, but the sternness of her voice was belied by the soft smile that touched her lips.

Dinner was a disaster. As was the custom in the Westcott household, all five daughters sat down to the table with their parents for the evening meal. Now Miss Tibbles did so as well. The Earl of Westcott tried to maintain his good humor, but it was difficult. Westcott liked to talk about horses, but after this afternoon that was scarcely a safe topic anymore. Still, he would not be cowed, he decided.

"Well, Diana, how is Lucky Lady?" Westcott asked, ignoring his wife's threatening stare.

Diana colored up to the roots of her hair. "Fine, Papa," she said, avoiding everyone's eyes.

Westcott pursed his lips. "And have you accustomed yourself to riding out with that new groom in attendance?" he persisted.

Diana all but choked on her food. "Yes, Papa," she said in a strangled voice.

Her four sisters watched Diana with scarcely concealed astonishment. Diana never lost her composure! She did just as she pleased and never allowed anyone or anything to get the better of her. Except today. And then Miss Tibbles made matters worse.

"I am not," she said, dabbing delicately at the corners of her mouth with her napkin, "generally in favor of encouraging girls to notice their male servants; however I should like to mention that I think Lady Diana's new groom, James is it?, possesses a most remarkable sense of humor."

Now everyone stared at Miss Tibbles. She refused to elaborate, however, and not one of the Westcotts dared ask her to do so. And, indeed, they had no chance for Miss Tibbles was already changing the subject.

"I understand you are shortly to be married, Lady Diana; my congratulations," Miss Tibbles said primly. "You have made a wise choice in the Duke of Berenford."

"Do you know the family?" Lady Westcott ventured to ask.

Miss Tibbles permitted herself a small smile. "I did attend his lordship's younger sister for a year and a half. She is quite a credit to me, now, I am happy to say."

"Will he like our Diana, do you think? The Duke of Berenford, I mean," Penelope asked.

Lady Westcott shot a sharp look at Penelope, but her daughter refused to see it. Fortunately, Miss Tibbles took the question in good part.

"Why should he not?" Miss Tibbles asked.

"Well, Diana is a bit unconventional," Barbara said hesitantly.

Diana blushed to the roots of her hair. Lady Westcott leapt to her aid. "What my daughter means, Miss Tibbles," the countess said, "is that we've raised Diana with a great deal of freedom. Strangers who don't know her as we do might not understand the levity and forcefulness in her nature."

Suddenly, Diana was tired of the entire discussion. "Why not say what you mean, Mama?" Diana said defiantly. "You are afraid that His Grace will take one look at me and turn tail, aren't you?"

There was a hint of bitterness in Diana's voice, and Lady Westcott hastened to reassure her. "I haven't the slightest doubt that the Duke of Berenford will take one look at you and fall straightway in love," Lady Westcott said with conviction.

"And even if he doesn't, he shall be too much the gentleman to cry off," Annabelle added placidly.

"In my opinion," Barbara said mischievously, "you ought to make certain, Diana, that he hasn't a chance to see you until your wedding day. Gentleman or not, no one would have the nerve to break off his engagement right at the altar."

"Yes, and we can lock the chapel door, if need be, and keep him there until the ceremony is done," the twins chimed in irrepressibly.

Diana's sisters didn't mean to be unkind. Had they any notion that the elder sister they considered so self-assured actually doubted her worth as a bride, they would never have spoken so heedlessly. But they had no idea that Diana stared into her mirror at night and wondered if the Duke of Berenford would come to hate the bargain he had made. Except for neighbors' sons who were so callow as not to count, no one had ever made Diana feel desirable. She knew only too well she was not the son her father wanted, nor the decorous daughter of her mother's dreams. She was neither fish nor fowl, but some odd creature in between, a curiosity, nothing more. And no man would ever see her for herself and still want her.

Except James. The name rose unbidden in Diana's mind, and for the third time her color rose. It was idiotic, it was ridiculous, it was foolish beyond permission to care what a mere groom thought of her. But Diana could not rid herself of the memory of his kiss and the knowledge that had stirred in her, the certainty, that this man had wanted to do far more.

Abruptly, Diana realized Miss Tibbles was speaking and that her voice was unexpectedly kind. "I think," she said with something of a twinkle in her eyes, "I can safely say that Berenford will be quite pleased with his bride. Charmed, in fact." When her pronouncement produced astonishment, Miss Tibbles added placidly, "Recollect that if Berenford wanted a meek chit to take to wife, he could have had his choice of dozens any time these past many years."

Once again the family could only stare, openmouthed, at

Miss Tibbles. This time it was Lady Westcott who changed the subject to something safely innocuous. And it was with relief, a short time later, that Lady Westcott rose to her feet and said, "Ladies, it is time we withdrew to the drawing room and left your father to his port. Miss Tibbles, you will join us, of course."

As the women about him rose, the Earl of Westcott shifted uneasily in his chair. "I should like a private word with Diana, and then we both shall join you," he said.

Lady Westcott hesitated, but she could see no harm in agreeing to the notion. Therefore she signified her approval with a curt nod of her head and then allowed her other four daughters to precede her from the room. Miss Tibbles calmly followed.

When they were gone, the Earl of Westcott stared at his daughter, suddenly uncertain how to go on. Diana stared back, a mixture of defiance, uncertainty, and unhappiness all mixed up in her expression. At last, the earl sighed. "I do want your happiness, you know, Diana," he said.

"I know, Papa," Diana agreed.

"Well, dash it all, you don't look happy," he protested.

Diana rose to her feet and began to pace about beside the table, almost as though she were a man. "How can you expect me to be happy?" she demanded. "I am shortly to marry a man I have never met."

The earl sighed. "We have been through this before, Diana. You agreed. The bargain has been made, the contracts signed. What is so terrible about marrying the Duke of Berenford?"

Abruptly, Diana sat down opposite her father and looked at him with such misery that it nearly broke his heart. "What if I can't be a good wife?" she asked. "What if he doesn't want me?"

Westcott stared at his eldest daughter. "What the devil is this nonsense?" he demanded with some alarm. "Even that damnable governess says Berenford will like you."

Diana looked away and then back again. A hint of desperation was in her voice as she tried to explain. "You've always let me run tame, Papa. What if I try to run tame with Berenford and he won't let me?"

Now the Earl of Westcott stared at his daughter impatiently. "I doubt Berenford will let you run tame, but no husband would. It's up to you to see that the pair of you rub along well together. I want to hear no more about it. Meanwhile, you'd best set your mind to thinking of what you want to take with you when you wed—other than Lucky Lady, of course."

"Yes, Papa." Diana sighed.

Out in the stables the Duke of Berenford was feeding the horses. He was no more happy than Lady Diana. He knew he had to leave, but he didn't want to. Berenford didn't want James to disappear. Or the Diana that James knew. What if she didn't like the Duke of Berenford nearly half so well as she liked the groom?

Chapter Eight

~

Diana went riding early the next morning. She waited only until they were out of sight of the stables before she drew Lucky Lady to a halt and turned to James. "I'm leaving for London tomorrow," she said without preamble. "I want to see Peter once more before I do."

James nodded curtly and changed direction to go with her to the cottage. The instant Lucky Lady and Devil appeared within sight of the cottage, Peter came running through the doorway, and both riders had to draw their horses up short not to run over him. James quirked an eyebrow at Diana and said, "I think Peter has recovered."

"I agree," Diana answered with a laugh. She slipped off her horse and handed the reins to James as she greeted the boy. "So, are we forgiven for clipping you?" she asked.

"Peter! Remember your manners," his mother called sharply from the doorway of the cottage.

Immediately, Diana moved toward her as Peter rushed past to feed the horses the lumps of sugar James had carried in his pocket.

"Is he truly all right?" Diana asked Peter's mother.

The woman nodded. "Right as rain. Happy as a grig when he saw you coming. Said you would, he did."

Now a shadow crossed Diana's face. "Unfortunately, I shan't be able to come again," she said. "I am leaving for London tomorrow. Perhaps James will be able to visit Peter in my stead."

The woman nodded, but had no time to reply, for Peter had come running back to his mother. There was a tone of awe in his voice as he said, "James told me he spoke to the head groom, up to the big house, and I'm to go any time I'm ready to be tried out to help."

Instinctively, Peter's mother looked to James, anxiety in her eyes and her voice as she replied, "That's very kind, but you're so young, Peter."

It was James who answered her. "He could come home every night, at least for now, and it needn't be every day," he said quietly. "Rawlins would take good care of Peter."

"But I want to go every day!" Peter protested.

His mother relented. He was growing quickly, she thought. Aloud she told James, doubtfully, "He does love horses. Will you be there to look after him as well?"

James hesitated, then shook his head. "I'm to go away tomorrow. When Lady Diana does. But Rawlins is a good man, I promise you."

Amid the short conversation that followed, Diana stood as though in shock. Was James coming to London, then? It seemed so unlikely. And yet, what else could he mean?

Soon thereafter they said good-bye to mother and son and rode to the stream that was Diana's favorite spot on the estate. Today she made no protest as he helped her dismount.

James tethered the horses to a nearby bush, then waited respectfully for Diana to speak, almost as though he knew she had something important to say. Indeed, had she not been so distracted, Diana might have thought he looked nervous. But as it was, she noticed nothing. Instead, she stared into the water and twisted her riding crop in her hand.

Finally, James cleared his throat. "Is something wrong, m'lady?" he asked.

Diana glanced over her shoulder at James and gave him half a smile. "It shouldn't be, I know. I'm going to London tomorrow."

"I know," James said. "I've heard."

Now Diana turned to face him. "Are you going with us?" she asked hopefully. "Is that what you meant when you told Peter's mother you were leaving tomorrow as well?"

James shook his head. It was his turn to look away. "Time I was moving on," he said uncomfortably.

"I see," Diana said, though she did not. Was he leaving because of her? Because she would be gone? It was a question Diana didn't dare ask. Instead, she said, "It was kind of you to ask Rawlins to take Peter on."

James shrugged. "He's a good lad and horse mad. He'll do well, I'm thinking."

Diana nodded. After a moment it was James's turn. "You don't seem happy to be going to London," he said.

"I should be," Diana countered.

"But you're not," James said, and it wasn't a question.

"No, I'm not," Diana agreed with a sigh.

"What is it that's got you so overset?" James asked gently. "You're to be married. To a duke and all. You'll have a title and all the fine things you choose. Isn't that what you want?" At her startled look he added hastily, "if it isn't too forward of me to be asking."

Diana hesitated. It was absurd to be speaking of such things with her groom and entirely improper. Yet, who else was there to talk with? Her parents had made it clear they were delighted to see her finally wed, and Annabelle was impatient for her turn. The younger girls were simply too young, and Miss Tibbles didn't bear thinking about. She tried to choose her words with care.

"I thought it would be enough to marry someone with the proper background, that I wouldn't care what he was like. Mama and Papa said that was the sensible thing to do since I hadn't fixed an interest on anyone else. But now, now I'm afraid I've made a terrible mistake. That it does matter what he's like," Diana said.

James drew her against his chest and rested his chin on the top of her head. "Would it be so terrible to go to London and see this duke of yours? Perhaps you'll discover you like him. And if not, if you think him an ogre, you can always cry off."

Now Diana pulled back and looked up at James. "Cry off?" she said slowly. "Sometimes you speak in the strangest way. For a groom, I mean," she amended.

James stood very stiff and still. What could he say? Part of him wanted desperately to tell Diana the truth, but part of him wanted her to go on thinking, for just a little longer, that he was only a groom. What if she didn't like the Duke of Berenford nearly as well as she liked James?

Diana mistook his silence. Mortified, she said, "Forgive me. I didn't mean to offend you. I have a wretched tongue, you know." She paused and tried to make light of the matter. "Perhaps his lordship, the Duke of Berenford, will take one look at me, listen to my conversation, and decide to cry off himself!"

Now James looked at her, and his voice was rough with some suppressed emotion as he said, "I doubt he's such a fool as to do that. He'll want to marry you the moment he claps eyes on you."

"Everyone seems so certain of that. You. Mama and Papa. Miss Tibbles. I wish I were so sure. Or that I wanted to be." Diana shook her head impatiently. She moved forward to lean against James's chest again, even though his arms were now straight at his side. "Hold me, James," she said softly. "I shan't ask anything else of you, but I need that."

Against his will, against every instinct that told him he was a fool to do so, James raised his arms and embraced Diana. When next they met, she might rain curses on his head, but for now he would hold her and give her the comfort she sought. And this time, when her lips searched for his, he did not evade them.

Chapter Nine

~

London was noisy and dirty and hedged about with even more rules than back at home, Diana thought crossly as she looked out the drawing room window of Lady Brisbane's house. It didn't matter that this room was elegantly appointed, as was her bedroom upstairs. It didn't matter that Lady Brisbane's staff saw to every conceivable comfort she and Mama could have wished. That they were staying in Lady Brisbane's house meant that there would be that many more eyes to witness the humiliation that was about to occur, if she cried off from her betrothal to the Duke of Berenford.

But Mama was implacable. "You must be presented to Society properly," Lady Westcott had said when Diana ventured to protest. "And one cannot do that from a hotel room. My sister knows everyone and has the space to give proper parties. Besides, I prefer the comfort of a house. And Ariana has a very comfortable house. It has more than enough room for all of us, even after your father brings the girls to London. And ever since Lord Brisbane's death three years ago, you know how lonely Ariana has been. Her son is off at war, and she needs to have us come stay with her."

Now Lady Westcott eyed her eldest daughter's back and said shrewdly, "Do stop staring out that window so gloomily, Diana, and come over here. I wish to speak with you about Almack's."

"Must we go?" Diana asked wearily.

Lady Westcott raised her eyebrows in an expression of well-bred astonishment. "You know very well that we must," she said. "And I think it very ungrateful of you to cavil at going, considering the trouble my sister went to in order to procure vouchers."

Lady Brisbane, who had been listening, preened a bit as she said, "I should venture to say that it is something of a coup to procure them in under a week."

Diana sighed and said, "A coup—for the daughter of an earl, who is betrothed to a duke? How could they refuse?"

"Now that is just what you don't understand," Lady Westcott said severely. "The patronesses of Almack's are a law unto themselves. They can and have withheld vouchers for girls, and gentlemen, whom one would have thought automatically ought to be allowed in. And you could be banned from there if you display such arrogance tonight. Or if you break any of the sacred rules. You do remember the sacred rules, don't you, Diana?" her mother demanded anxiously.

"Yes, Mama," Diana said, weary, and began to recite them and concluded with one of the most sacred of all. ". . . And I must not waltz until given permission."

"Very good," her mother said, approving. "But don't, I pray you, display such a gloomy face tonight. Whatever will the Duke of Berenford say if he sees you like this? He will think you don't wish to be married."

Suddenly, Diana sat up straighter. "Is Berenford to be there, then?" she asked with anxiety.

Lady Westcott hesitated, but decided it would be best not to lie to her daughter. Better to give the girl some time to accept the notion. "Yes, I have had a brief letter from him saying that he means to be there and hopes to dance with you tonight."

Diana's hand stole to her throat. "He is in London? He means to be there tonight?"

"I have just said so," Lady Westcott said with some exasperation. "Really, Diana, have your wits gone begging?"

Diana turned back to the window, and her voice was toneless as she said, "I'm sorry, Mama. Somehow I just did not think I would have to face him so soon—or in such a public place. I . . . I thought he might come here."

"So soon?" Lady Westcott echoed incredulously. "You think this soon? I thought to see him the day after we arrived in London. Although I must say I am grateful we have had the extra time to repair the deficiencies of your wardrobe. This way the duke will see you to your best advantage. As for meeting you in a public place, no doubt that is part of Berenford's consideration. He knows the initial meeting will be awkward for you. At least in public there will be others about to talk with and dancing to do so that you might become better acquainted with him. Yes, it is just the sort of consideration I would have expected from Berenford. You need expect no awkward scenes from him, demanding intimacies you do not wish to allow."

"No, of course not," Diana replied dully, thinking of the impertinent groom, James, who had demanded just such intimacies. An ache of loneliness swept through her. Diana stared out the window and wondered where James was and what he was doing right now.

* * *

James was damning his tailor for a jacket that fit too tightly as he faced his mother in the drawing room of her London town house. Suddenly, the heavy wine draperies seemed oppressive and the furniture too numerous as he nearly tripped over a chair.

The Duchess of Berenford's expression did not change in the slightest as she watched her son enter the room. Beneath her fingers the heavy green satin of her skirt was crushed as she tightened her grip upon it, determined not to let him see how anxious she was. To that end her voice was cool as she said, "Well, Jeremy? Are you through with games? Your bride-to-be, the Lady Diana, is in London. Do you mean to call upon her? People are beginning to talk, you know. And after your disappearance for weeks, well, I didn't know what to tell them."

As she concluded this little speech, the Duchess of Berenford shrugged one elegant shoulder and sniffed. The Duke of Berenford eyed her coldly. He knew only too well this mood his mother was in.

"I have told you," Berenford said in a voice that betrayed none of his inner consternation, "I had pressing business out of town. As for what you should say, well," he said, shrugging his own elegantly clad shoulder, "I see no reason why you should have to say anything. Why should anyone expect you to know where I am or what I might be doing?"

The duchess shot her son a look of cold anger. "You are my son. I am expected to know everything."

"Fools," Berenford said succinctly.

The duchess bristled. "You are evading the point, Jeremy. What do you mean to do about Lady Diana?

Berenford flicked an invisible speck of lint off his sleeve. "Do? I shall dance with her tonight at Almack's and tomorrow I shall call upon her at home."

"Oughtn't you to do that in the opposite order?" his mother asked with a frown. "Won't it look strange that she can't recognize you?"

An odd light came into Berenford's eyes at her words, and he smiled. "Ah, but I can recognize her," he said softly. "And it may well be that she will not find me such a stranger as you think."

These very curious words caused the Duchess of Berenford to straighten up in alarm. "Jeremy James Stowall, what have you been up to?" she demanded.

Berenford looked at his mother coolly. "I?" he asked. "I have been doing what I must." He paused and sighed. "Never fear, Mother. Lady Diana and I shall be married just as our families arranged. Now you must excuse me. I have much to do this afternoon."

With a strong sense of disquiet, the Duchess of Berenford watched her son leave the room. She hoped he wasn't going to be difficult like his father sometimes had been. It was a good thing, she thought, that she had the strength to rule both of them properly. But she did wish she knew what Jeremy intended to do this afternoon. She mistrusted that look upon his face. As a boy, it had always meant he was planning mischief.

What Jeremy, the ninth Duke of Berenford, was doing was arranging for flowers to be sent round to his betrothed, as Diana could have told her that evening. The sight of the mass of blooms ought to have reassured her, she thought, but they did not. Diana could not help thinking they were a sign of the Duke of Berenford's intent to carry through on their marriage, and she was not in the least certain she wished to do so. If only he had called on her in private, then Diana might have been able to talk with him frankly.

As it was, their first meeting must be entirely too public, with far too many interested eyes upon them. How could she draw back under those circumstances?

It was not surprising, therefore, that Diana set forth with her mother and her aunt in a state of some trepidation that evening. To be sure, she looked wonderful in the dress of pale rose silk that had arrived only that morning, along with gloves and shoes. She ought to have glowed with self-confidence. Instead, Diana found herself half wishing she looked a fright so that Berenford might cry off.

Still, it was impossible to suppress a sense of excitement as she stepped across the threshold of that sacred establishment, Almack's. Here was where futures were made or destroyed, and here was where hers would begin.

At her side, Lady Brisbane smiled with satisfaction. "He's here," she told her niece. "Your betrothed, the Duke of Berenford is approaching us."

"Goodness, he looks just like his father," Lady Westcott said with surprise as she spotted Berenford.

Slowly, Diana turned to see the man who was to marry her. Her eyes widened. She gripped her mother's arm painfully hard. And the room began to spin around her. The next thing Diana knew, she was lying on the floor with far too many faces above her.

"The heat," Lady Brisbane said hastily, "it has overcome her."

Lady Westcott bent her face close to Diana's. A hint of desperation in her voice, she hissed, "Wake up, Diana! You are drawing every eye! Wake up before you create an even greater scandal!"

Instinctively, Diana responded to the command. She forced herself to a sitting position, ignoring the dizziness that threatened to overwhelm her. She was not a fool. Tomorrow tongues would be wagging all over London, and she must do what she could to minimize the damage.

In the same sort of coolly detached voice that she had often heard her aunt, Lady Brisbane, use, Diana said, "How absurd of me. I tripped on my hem and must have hit my head when I fell. Mama, will you help me rise?"

And then, to Lady Westcott's relief, Diana was on her feet, smiling as if nothing had occurred and turning to greet the Duke of Berenford. Lady Brisbane hastened to introduce them.

"Diana, my love, this is the Duke of Berenford. Your Grace, how delightful to see you this evening. May I present my niece, Diana."

But Berenford was not looking at Lady Brisbane. His eyes were fixed on Diana, his color as pale as her own as he bent over her hand and brought it to his lips. "It is my pleasure to meet you, Lady Diana," he said.

Diana wanted to snatch her hand away, but there were far too many people watching with malicious little smiles of satisfaction. She had already given them too much to talk about. So now Diana greeted Berenford with all the appearance of pleasure that she could muster. "Good evening, Your Grace. What a delightful surprise to see you here."

Berenford let out the breath he had been holding. She was not going to make a scene. Everything was going to be all right.

"Shall we dance?" he asked formally.

Something like panic flared in Diana's eyes, then they narrowed, and she said, almost with a purr, "It is a waltz, and I have not yet been given permission."

But Lady Jersey was nearby, drawn by the fuss when Diana had fainted, and she hastened to say, "Ah, but I give you permission, my dear."

Diana looked at Berenford. She could see no way out of it. Very well, she would dance with him, but he would, she thought, regret it. So Diana took the hand Berenford held out to her and allowed him to lead her out onto the dance floor. As they whirled about the room, she spoke softly, but with a voice that cut like a knife.

"How nice to see you, James, dressed as something other than a groom. Though I must say that you seemed more at home with the horses."

"I was," Berenford replied. That startled Diana, and she looked up at him. He smiled and added, "At least there I did not have to watch my feet as I tried to talk with you."

Delight raced through Diana at the warmth in his tone, but she ruthlessly suppressed it. She would not allow herself to be charmed. Curtly, she said, "What a laugh you must have had at our expense! Did we amuse you, Your Grace?"

Berenford's voice was low and earnest as he replied, "I never laughed at you, Diana."

Suddenly, a thought occurred to her, and she almost missed a step. "Did my father recognize you?" Diana asked suspiciously.

Berenford hesitated. "I think perhaps he did," Berenford said slowly. "Though he couldn't seem to decide if I was myself masquerading as a groom or if I was one of my father's by-blows."

Now anger kindled in Diana's eyes. "Why didn't he tell me?" she growled.

"Perhaps because he wanted us to become better acquainted?" Berenford suggested. "Or because if I was a by-blow, he didn't wish to speak of such things to you?"

"But you have no such hesitation," Diana replied, a martial gleam in her eyes.

Berenford smiled down at her with such affection that Diana felt herself blush. "Ah, but perhaps I, or rather the humble groom, James, knows you well enough to know you would prefer plain speaking."

Abruptly, Diana remembered her anger at him. She said stiffly, "I won't marry you. Not after the trick you pulled."

For a long moment Berenford stared down at Diana, taking in the tilt of her chin, the look in her eyes, the defiance in her voice. When he spoke, his own voice was cool as he said, "You have no choice. It is too late to cry off, as my mother has already pointed out to me."

Now Diana did miss a step. "*You* wanted to cry off?" she demanded.

Berenford smiled. "No. But my mother reminded me, nevertheless."

She would not be flummoxed by his smile, she would not be! Diana told herself desperately. Aloud, she said, "Well I, for one, am not so concerned by what the world might say. I will not marry a man who would serve me such a trick as you did. It was unforgivable."

"Quite unforgivable," Berenford agreed meekly. "But I still want you to marry me."

"But why?" Diana asked, a hint of desperation in her voice. "Why do you want to marry me?"

Berenford smiled even wider. There was a warm light in his eyes as he looked down at Diana and said softly, "Do you really not know? If we were not in the middle of the dance floor, I would remind you with a kiss."

Now Diana flushed. It was too much. Berenford had humiliated her with his masquerade as a groom. Diana found herself remembering only too well the feel of his lips on hers, his hands roaming where they ought not to have roamed. Worse, she found herself wanting it to happen again.

Suddenly, Diana could not bear it any longer. Oblivious to the stares about them, Diana pulled free and fled, leaving Berenford standing alone in the middle of the dance floor. With her head held high, Diana strode to where her mother stood watching with an appalled look upon her face and said, "Mama, I have the headache. I wish to go home."

Lady Brisbane started to remonstrate. One look at her daughter's face, however, told Lady Westcott it would do no good. Instead, she hastily turned to her sister and said loudly, so that those nearby could overhear, "The poor girl is not used to these hours. Or the city yet. Come, dear, I'll take you home. You'll feel much the thing tomorrow."

And with a determined smile Lady Westcott led her daughter out of Almack's, followed by Lady Brisbane, who took care to drop an amiable word here and there.

Only when they were in the carriage did Lady Brisbane turn to Diana and demand, "Are you trying to ruin yourself? What on earth were you thinking, leaving Berenford in the middle of the dance floor?"

But Diana did not answer her aunt. Instead, she looked at her mother and said, "Did you not recognize him, Mama? He was the impertinent groom."

"Groom?" Lady Westcott said, bewildered. "Of course he is to be your bridegroom. And I recognized that Berenford looks like his father. But what do you mean he was impertinent?"

Diana sighed with exasperation. "Not bridegroom. Groom! He was the groom, James, back home. From the stables. Didn't Papa tell you?"

Now an annoyed glint came into Lady Westcott's eyes as she replied, "Your father didn't tell me a thing, and I still don't understand. You know I don't ride and never go out to the stables anyway."

So Diana explained precisely what the Duke of Berenford had done, or a censored version, at any rate, and her father's part in this. When she was finished, Lady Westcott and Lady Brisbane were both aghast. But they did not see matters quite as Diana expected.

"I shall have a few things to say to your father when he arrives in London," Lady Westcott said grimly. "And to Berenford when he comes to call."

"But I don't want him to call," Diana said. "Don't you understand? I want to cry off."

Lady Brisbane fixed her niece with a piercing gaze that matched the implacable edge to her voice. "Even if we were to allow you to cry off, you would need to see Berenford to do so in private. But you cannot, you will not, be so foolish as to do so."

"Your aunt is quite right," Lady Westcott said decisively. "You cannot cry off now."

"But Mama, think of what he did!" Diana protested.

"I *am* thinking of it!" Lady Westcott replied. "My God, Diana! You rode out with Berenford, alone, every day he was there. If anyone were to find out, you would be ruined! You must marry Berenford."

Diana's eyes widened. "I can ride out with a groom and everyone approves, but if I ride out with Berenford, I am ruined?" she demanded incredulously.

"I know it sounds absurd," Lady Brisbane said with some exasperation, "but there it is."

"Diana, think!" Lady Westcott added. "You were alone, both of you, in the country. Anything could have happened. That is what people will say. A servant wouldn't dare take liberties, but a duke, well, it will be assumed something havey-cavey was going on, yes, and assumed that your father and I knew all about it. We will all be ruined if word gets out! Diana, you must marry him now."

"You keep saying that," Diana said quietly, "but I won't be sacrificed on the altar of propriety. I would rather be ruined."

Now Lady Brisbane was truly angry. "You are saying so only because you haven't the faintest idea what it really means," she said with patent exasperation. "But even if you did, you are being truly selfish. Don't you understand? It would not be only yourself you ruined but your entire family."

"Winsborough would cry off," Lady Westcott said in a ghastly voice as she conjured up the image, "leaving Annabelle in the lurch, and you would be ruining Barbara and the twins' futures as well. Is that what you wish to do?"

"No, Mama," Diana said with a sigh.

"Good," Lady Brisbane said, leaning back against the squabs. "Then we will say no more about it. Berenford will come to call, and your mother will speak to him, quite sharply, I assure you. And the wedding will go on as planned."

That, Diana took leave to doubt. But this time she kept her thoughts to herself. Once she found a way out of this mess, then she would present the *fait accompli* to Mama and to her aunt. For now she would silently contemplate every revenge she could think of toward the Duke of Berenford.

Chapter Ten

The Duke of Berenford hesitated on the top step of the house where Lady Westcott and Diana were staying in London. Would they receive him? He wondered. How could they not? The question was, would Diana cry off. It would be a long time before Berenford forgot the humiliation of being abandoned on the dance floor or the whispered comments that had followed him about the room after.

With grim determination Berenford mounted the last step and rapped on the front door. It was opened by an impeccable footman who, upon learning his identity, allowed that both Lady Westcott and her daughter were at home to *him*.

Berenford was left to cool his heels in the small drawing room. He looked around. It was done in silver and green with furniture in the Egyptian motif. He sniffed. Lady Brisbane was a bit out of date, but he would not be the one to tell her so.

Then they entered. Lady Brisbane came first, followed by Lady Westcott. At the moment Diana was nowhere to be seen. Berenford lifted one eyebrow in surprise. Instantly, Lady Brisbane was on the offensive.

"Don't look at me that way, Berenford! You shall see

Diana shortly. But first her mother and I have something to say to you. What the devil do you mean by masquerading as a groom and compromising my niece?"

Berenford stared at her coldly. So Diana had told them. Well, there was nothing to do but brazen it out. He lifted both eyebrows now as he said coolly, "I wished to appraise my bride beforehand, and I did. She will be quite satisfactory, I believe. As for compromising her, nonsense! We are betrothed. In a month we will be married. In any event, unless you tell them, people need never know what occurred."

Lady Brisbane tilted her head to one side for a moment, then nodded as though satisfied. Lady Westcott, however, still had her doubts. "Diana said, that is, she seems somewhat reluctant . . . I mean to say that she needs to be reassured that you, well, she seems to have it in her head you were mocking her."

Berenford had no difficulty understanding this tangled sentence. Mercifully, he cut Lady Westcott short and said, "I shall do everything in my power to persuade your daughter that I was not mocking her and that I do mean to marry her. Now, if I may speak with Lady Diana? Alone?"

Lady Westcott hesitated and looked at her sister. Lady Brisbane sighed in exasperation. "Oh, Delwinia, we might as well let him speak with her. What else are we to do? If she cries off now, it will be a scandal. And perhaps he can manage her where we cannot."

Lady Westcott nodded and went to fetch her daughter. While she was gone, Lady Brisbane looked at Berenford and said, "My niece will need careful handling, you know. I trust you will not muck things up further."

Berenford bowed. "I shall do my best," he replied coolly, even as he inwardly seethed. Damn Diana for putting him in this intolerable position!

His annoyance was forgotten, however, the moment Diana appeared. Today she looked nothing like the hoyden-ish tomboy James had followed about the estate. Instead, she was elegant in figured green satin. Her hair had been cut and curled, and someone had been teaching Diana how to glide across a room rather than move as if she were stomping across the moors.

Jeremy/James did not even realize he was holding his breath until Diana came to a halt, two feet in front of him, and he let it out. "You're beautiful!" he said without thinking.

Diana lifted an eyebrow, her expression unchanged, giving no hint of the turmoil she felt inside. "Spanish coin, Your Grace?" she asked.

"No, only the truth," Berenford said hoarsely.

Diana allowed her gaze to travel up and down. Then, with a mocking smile she said, "We both seem very different in our new feathers. It seems that clothes make both the man and the woman."

Jeremy winced. "I'm sorry," he said softly.

Diana lifted her shoulder in an elegant little shrug. Behind them, however, Lady Brisbane gave a romantic sigh. "I think, Delwinia, that we may safely leave them alone," she said.

Lady Westcott hesitated. She knew only too well the look upon Diana's face, and it did not bode well for the betrothal. Still, there was something else there as well, and that gave her hope.

"You may have twenty minutes," Lady Westcott said in an austere voice to both Diana and Berenford.

Diana turned to ask what her mother meant and saw with dismay that both she and Lady Brisbane were already withdrawing from the room. "Wait, don't go!" she cried.

Both women paused. "Really, Diana," Lady Brisbane said with some exasperation, "His Grace is a gentleman, and the pair of you are betrothed. Your desire for propriety is very commendable, but this once I think we might dispense with the formality of a chaperone."

Behind her Berenford's voice came soft and taunting as he said, "Afraid?"

Diana whirled to face him. "Not in the least," she said stiffly.

"Good. Then come and sit with me," Berenford commanded, holding out a hand to her.

Gingerly, Diana put her hand in his and allowed him to lead her to the sofa. Neither one noticed as Lady Brisbane and Lady Westcott left the room.

When they were settled, Berenford leaned forward as if to kiss Diana. Instantly, her hand went up between them to hold him off. "No!" she said.

Jeremy arched an eyebrow. "But you liked it so well, back home. I thought I would remind you how well matched we are."

Diana's face flushed scarlet. "You are a beast to remind me!" she said.

"Am I?" Berenford replied. "Why? Would you rather it had not been me, but only a groom? Someone you could make your toy and then dispense with when you came to London? Do you mean to say you don't wish to enjoy your husband's, that is to say, my, embrace?"

Diana rose to her feet and began to pace the room. "You don't understand," she said, her hands clasping and unclasping in patent agitation. "You deceived me."

"As you meant to deceive Berenford?" he suggested harshly.

"No!" Diana turned to face the duke. "I meant to break

things off with him, that is to say, you. That is to say, unless I found him, you, amiable and the sort of man I could respect and love."

Now Berenford rose to his feet, every inch the duke. "I see. You could not marry a groom, so you meant to consider very carefully whether Berenford came up to the mark. Just as you said you would, when you talked with James."

"I told you why," Diana said, a plea in her voice.

Berenford nodded. "So you did. And I understood then, just as I understand now. Indeed, what I fail to see is the cause for your agitation. I am Berenford, our marriage is still eminently suitable, and we have enjoyed a good joke," he said.

"Joke?" Diana echoed the word incredulously. "You think this a joke? Do you know how many hours I worried over what we did, James and I? Whether I had betrayed my family, His Grace the Duke of Berenford, and myself? Do you know how many times I cried myself to sleep this past week?"

Diana stopped and drew a breath. She must not shriek at Berenford. She must, somehow, retain her dignity. She took a step toward him.

"Do you not understand?" she asked. "I did not know who you were. I thought you were, in fact, the groom you pretended to be. I called myself wanton for allowing you to take such liberties with me. And I called myself ten kinds of fool for allowing myself to care for a groom, to even consider casting fortune to the winds and running off with you."

Delight lit Berenford's words, and he took a step toward Diana. "Really? You thought of running off with me?" he asked.

Diana hastily took a step to the side, evading Berenford. "You still think it a joke! But I did not. I had to worry about how I would confess to Berenford what I had done. Or whether I should simply cry off, regardless of scandal. I had to worry that I was placing in jeopardy every trust my family placed in me, not only to remember propriety, but also to marry well so that the family would not be disgraced. I had to feel the terror that I was coming to London to face my future, and I would hate it. That was scarcely a lark to me."

Berenford was aghast. Diana could see it on his face. Even his voice shook as he said, "I didn't mean for it to be that way. I didn't think."

Diana caught him up on those words and pressed her attack. "No, you didn't think, did you? It was a lark for you. A few weeks to play at being a groom, always knowing you had your own home, your own role as duke to return to. What difference did it make to you if we went further than we ought? You knew we were to be married. You knew my parents would understand if we were caught embracing by the stream. You knew that all you would have to do was give them your true name. But I didn't know. And I was terribly afraid."

Now Diana was trembling, and Berenford reached to take her in his arms. Again she stepped farther away. "No," Diana said. "I won't let you touch me. I came in here only to tell you our betrothal is off. I won't marry you. Not after you deceived me as you did. The only question to decide is whether you shall send the notice to the papers or whether I shall be the one to do so."

"No."

That one word was implacable in its finality. Diana

gawked at Berenford. She blinked. Surely, she had not heard him aright.

"No?" she echoed uncertainly.

"Neither of us shall send such a notice," he said, crossing his arms across his chest just as James, the groom, had once done.

"This is absurd," Diana fumed. "You cannot mean for everyone to go on thinking we are to be married."

"That is precisely what I mean," Berenford said coolly, "since it is no more or less than the truth."

Diana stared at him and blinked. "Didn't you hear me?" she demanded. "I said I refuse to marry you."

Berenford stared back. "I heard. I simply disagree. You will marry me. You have no choice. To cry off now would ruin both of us."

Diana stamped her foot. "You cannot be so absurd!" she cried. "I can understand my mother and my aunt saying so, but you know better. After the initial furor, and all the gossip that we both shall have to weather, the *ton* will find another scandal to talk about. You are a duke, and I am the well-dowered daughter of an earl. You are too intelligent to believe that either of us shall have any difficulty finding another partner."

He sighed, and that sigh, so full of weariness, touched Diana in spite of her determination not to be swayed by anything Berenford said or did. Now he turned his back on her, and Diana almost reached out her hand to stop him.

Over his shoulder Berenford tossed his reply. "You think it will be so easy for us to find other partners? We, who were reduced to the circumstance already of each agreeing to marry someone we had never met?"

Diana winced. "I had all but forgotten that," she said in a small voice. Then she straightened her shoulders and added, "But that is nothing to the point. I tell you I wish to be released from our betrothal."

Over his shoulder Berenford asked, "Not even if I promise to be the gentleman James was not? At least until after we are married?"

Diana stared at his back. A gentleman? Not her James? Not the impertinent groom who had kissed her? A sense of loss gripped Diana, and she took a step backward, for otherwise she would have reached out to touch Berenford. Desperately, Diana reminded herself of the nights she had cried herself to sleep softly into the pillow so her sisters would not hear. If he could cause her such distress before they were wed, how deeply would he hurt her after, never thinking of the effect his behavior would have?

Abruptly, Diana realized Berenford was still waiting for his answer. "A perfect gentleman?" she repeated. "I cannot picture such a thing. In any event, I still wish to be released from our betrothal."

Slowly, Berenford turned around. His face was almost harsh in its stillness, and he betrayed none of the hope he felt at the forlorn sounds he heard in her voice. "Ah," he said gently, "but I can and will be such a gentleman. As for our betrothal, I do not choose to release you. And if you send such a notice to the papers, I shall refute it. Quite, quite publicly."

Diana stared at the duke. She was too intelligent not to realize what it would mean if he was to do as he said. Bewildered, she shook her head as she asked, "But why? Why do you persist in wanting to marry me?"

A small smile turned up the corners of Berenford's mouth. He came toward Diana, and this time she did not run from him, not even when he took her hands in his and lifted first one to his lips and then the other. Indeed, Diana seemed mesmerized by the warmth in his eyes and the way they twinkled down at her as he said, "Because a certain groom I know has fallen hopelessly, irretrievably, endlessly in love with you, and I cannot bear to break his heart."

She ought to back away from him, to pull her hands free and send him on his way. That was what Diana told herself. But she could not. She still stood frozen, her hands in Berenford's, when the door of the small drawing room opened and Lady Brisbane and Lady Westcott tiptoed back into the room. It was Lady Brisbane's voice that broke the spell.

"How delightful! You've patched things up, have you? Good. That's all right and tight, then," she said.

Instantly, Diana snatched her hands free from Berenford's. "No! That is, nothing is decided."

"Nothing?" Lady Westcott asked with something of a wail. "Oh, Diana!"

Only Berenford seemed unmoved. He continued to look down at Diana with the same twinkle in his eyes until she blushed. In a deep, husky voice he asked her, "Could we say that we have decided not yet to decide? To go on, for the moment, as though we are still betrothed and the wedding still to be in one month?"

She ought to refuse, Diana knew it. It was dishonest to do otherwise. But she could not refuse. Not when Berenford looked down at her like that, and every inch of her ached to throw herself against his chest and cling to him. But Diana could not do that either. Instead, she lifted her chin and said in as calm a voice as she could command, "Yes, I think we might do that."

And then both Lady Brisbane and Lady Westcott fluttered about, offering congratulations.

"Most sensible," Lady Brisbane said approvingly.

"Dearest, how pleased I am for you! It will all work out, you'll see," Lady Westcott cried as she embraced her daughter.

"What do you mean to tell your mother?" Lady Brisbane asked Berenford dryly. "She will wish to know when the party is to be given to publicly acknowledge the betrothal."

Now Berenford looked distinctly uncomfortable once more. He tugged at his cravat and looked everywhere, save at Diana. There was, however, no evading matters.

"My, uh, mother wished to discuss precisely that point with you this afternoon," Berenford said unhappily.

"This afternoon!" Lady Westcott cried.

"My dear boy, you should have told us at once. There are matters to be attended to if we are to call upon your mother this afternoon," Lady Brisbane said severely.

"Yes, well, she wanted you to call this afternoon, but I persuaded her that a few days from now would be better," Berenford said. "I expect she will be sending round her summons, er, invitation shortly."

His audience gave a collective sigh of relief. "Does your mother know what you did?" Lady Westcott asked.

Berenford distinctly shuddered. "No," he said. "And it is my devout hope that she never finds out."

Lady Westcott nodded sympathetically, but Lady Brisbane's eyes narrowed, and she was quick to press the advantage. "Then you had best be very nice to Diana these coming weeks, hadn't you?" Lady Brisbane asked Berenford, pinning him with her shrewd gaze.

That, however, was going too far. Berenford drew himself up to his full height and took Diana's hand in his. He was pleased to note she gave it willingly and that it did not tremble. Then Berenford looked directly at Diana as he replied in a voice that began coldly, but almost at once softened to a gentle tone.

"I shall indeed do my best to be kind to Diana, to please her in every way that I can. Not because I am commanded to do so," Jeremy said, gazing into Diana's eyes, "but because it is my dearest wish to do so. I have begun badly, I know, but it is my dearest wish to prove to Diana that I mean to make her a good and loving husband."

"How prettily said," Lady Westcott murmured with a romantic sigh.

"If he means it," Lady Brisbane added dryly. Then, more briskly, she went on to say, "Even if he does not, at least he has the intelligence to pretend. You'll do, Berenford. My niece will come round, and the pair of you will make a satisfactory match of it, after all."

Berenford stared at Lady Brisbane frostily. He would do? Satisfactory match? The most eligible bachelor in London? "I am gratified to meet with your approval, Lady Brisbane," he said with icy irony.

But Lady Brisbane was undaunted. "Don't look at me like that," she countered calmly. "I have been acquainted with your mother since you were in leading strings, Berenford. She is a most sensible woman, and I can only hope that you have grown into an equally sensible son."

Diana pressed back a giggle at the indignation she could sense in every line of James's, no, Jeremy's body. "Never mind my aunt," she told him soothingly. "She cannot help but try to manage everyone."

That brought Berenford back to himself. He looked down at Diana and smiled. "I shall see you tomorrow," he promised. "We shall go out riding in the morning, just as we did in the country."

"No!" two voices cried out at once.

"You cannot," Lady Brisbane said imperiously. "I forbid it."

That set up Berenford's back, and he was about to tell her he would do as he wished when Lady Westcott's voice forestalled him. In a gentle, reproachful manner she said, "Surely you have not thought it out, Berenford. What if someone were to discover you had masqueraded as Diana's groom? The very worst thing you could do would be to be seen riding with her. And yes, I know the possibility is remote, but do you really wish to take the risk? Besides, we did not bring Diana's mount to London. Can you not take her out for a drive tomorrow afternoon, instead?"

Reluctantly, Berenford admitted the wisdom of Lady Westcott's words. Still, he looked to Diana for her reply. She looked at him wistfully as she said with a sigh, "I suppose Mama has the right of it. Dearly as I should like a gallop, I suppose that would not be in order in any event. And rather than ride tamely, as I suppose I must, on some hired hack, I think I should prefer to ride in a carriage. It would remind me less of Lucky Lady and what I am missing, here in London."

Berenford lifted her hand to his lips. "Whatever you wish," he said. "Tomorrow at five."

And then, before anyone could set any more commands upon him, or ask any more questions, Berenford took his leave. Nothing was going as planned, and yet, he thought, a spring coming to his step, there was hope. Where, he wondered, was the nearest florist?

It was understandable to Berenford, now that Diana had explained matters to him, that she should have certain qualms. But Berenford intended to erase those qualms as quickly as he could. To that end, he wished to place an order for roses—masses and masses of roses. Perhaps a few other flowers as well. He would overwhelm Diana with various kindnesses, he thought, and then she would soon see she was lucky to be marrying him after all.

Chapter Eleven

~

The next afternoon, Diana, her mother, and Lady Brisbane had just sat down to a neat little nuncheon when suddenly the house seemed to fill with the sound of squealing girls, a much put upon father, and servants hauling trunks into the entryway. There could be no doubt as to who had arrived. Lady Westcott preceded her sister and daughter into the foyer by only a few steps.

"Adam! You've come early!" she cried.

Lord Westcott caught his wife up into his arms and bussed her soundly, oblivious to all the eyes that were watching them. "I thought to surprise you, my love," he said. He paused, and his eyes rested a moment on Diana as he added smoothly, "Besides, I wished to see for myself that everything was going well here in London. That there was no difficulty about the betrothal between Diana and the Duke of Berenford."

Lady Westcott, who was all too conscious of the eyes upon them, hastily pulled free. She patted her hair back into place as she said, "Difficulty? There is no difficulty. But never mind that. I am delighted to see you, Adam. And the girls. How was your journey?"

The girls were in the best of spirits. They had, none of

them, ever been to London before, and their voices immediately rose in argument as to which of the sights must be
first to be seen. Instantly, Miss Tibbles's calm, imperious
voice cut across the uproar.

"This journey to London is in no way a reason to abandon lessons. I shall expect the girls to attend to their
lessons, as usual, each morning."

Now three pairs of incredulous eyes turned toward Miss
Tibbles while the elder sisters looked at one another in consternation. Even Lady Westcott was moved to say, somewhat timidly, "Yes, but surely while they are here, the girls
ought to be allowed to see something of the city."

Miss Tibbles sniffed. "I suppose, if they are good," she
said reluctantly, "I could agree that it would be to the benefit of their education to be shown some of the more improv-
ing sights of the city."

A cheer went up, but one glance from Miss Tibbles was
sufficient to cut it short. With unaccustomed meekness, the
twins and Barbara and Annabelle allowed themselves to be
directed to go upstairs with Lady Brisbane's footman to be
shown where they might wash up before they sat down to
nuncheon.

Lady Westcott watched all of this, shaking her head in
astonishment. "You've accomplished miracles, Miss Tibbles," she said.

"I told you she would," Lady Brisbane said with satisfaction.

Miss Tibbles was tranquil as she replied, "They are good
girls and only needed a proper direction for their spirits. I
have provided one. Now, if you will excuse me, it would be
best if I supervise matters myself."

Then she, too, went up the stairs. Lady Westcott and
Lady Brisbane followed, conversing amiably as to the best

disposition of the rooms for the girls. Besides which, both ladies were desirous of seeing for themselves the methods Miss Tibbles used to accomplish such an extraordinary transformation in Lady Westcott's daughters. That left Lord Westcott and Diana facing one another as the servants began to carry the luggage up the stairs.

Diana drew her father into the small parlor off the entryway and shut the door. There she confronted him. "Why didn't you tell me James was the Duke of Berenford?" Diana demanded. "And don't tell me you didn't know, for Mama recognized Berenford at once, and if she recognized him, then you must have done so as well."

In a strangled voice Westcott asked, "Your mother recognized James as the Duke of Berenford?"

Impatiently, Diana said, "No, Mama recognized Berenford at Almack's. She never saw James at home because she never went to the stables. But you did. Often. And if Mama knew what Berenford looked like, so must you have known. Why didn't you tell me?"

As Westcott looked about, obviously searching for some way to pacify her, Diana advanced on her father, causing him to hastily retreat behind a chair. Why, he reflected bitterly, couldn't she be as meek as her sister Annabelle?

"But don't you like Berenford?" Westcott temporized. "Isn't he an excellent rider?"

Diana continued to advanced on her father, and he moved to another chair. "That, Papa, is beside the point. Why didn't you tell me?"

"I wanted you to discover it for yourself?" Westcott suggested hopefully, still moving. Diana glared at him, and he tried again. "I hoped Berenford would tell you himself? I thought it his duty to do so?"

Diana shook her head. She stopped advancing on her father and crossed her arms over her chest. Useless to press him. He would only offer words that he thought she would accept. Instead, Diana tried a new direction with her words.

"Do you know," she said cheerfully, "that when I discovered who Berenford was, I was so appalled, so stunned, that I disgraced myself in public? And broke off the betrothal?"

"But your mother said there was no difficulty. That everything was fine," Westcott protested.

Diana smiled, determined to extract the maximum effect from her words. "Did she? I suppose she will persist in believing fairy tales."

Westcott mopped his forehead with a slightly trembling hand. "And Berenford? He agreed to end the betrothal? The announcement has been sent?"

Diana took pity on her father, even as she told herself sternly that he deserved none. "No," she said with a sigh, "Berenford has persuaded me to give him a little time to convince me I still wish to marry him."

"And he has sent Diana masses of roses," Lady Brisbane said, advancing into the room. As Diana shot her a look of dislike, Lady Brisbane told her, "Don't you glare at me, my girl! You are the one who left the door slightly ajar so that the entire household has heard this conversation. Or would have, had I not had the wisdom to send them all about on errands and close the door more firmly. But do not try to tell me it is none of my affair. I helped your mother, and father of course, settle on Berenford as an eligible *parti* for you. And I am the one who lives in London and will have to hear whatever gossip your behavior provokes. So you see, I do have an interest in this matter."

"Roses?" Westcott said, his face brightening as he seized on the word. "That's a good sign. Must mean he likes the gel, don't you think?"

"Since he was practically on his knees, begging her to marry him yesterday, one might think so," Lady Brisbane replied dryly.

All at once, it was too much for Diana. She whirled on her heel and headed for her room upstairs. She could not, would not, discuss Berenford with any member of her family, she vowed.

Unfortunately, Diana could not keep her vow. She was met at the top of the stairs by Barbara, who dragged her into her room where Annabelle, Rebecca, and Penelope were all waiting for her.

"What is Berenford like?" Rebecca asked. "Is he handsome?"

"Does he mean to let you go your own way?" Penelope asked, a hint of anxiety in her voice.

"Did he kiss you?" Barbara demanded outrageously. "And did you kiss him back?"

"Is he acceptable to you?" Annabelle asked quietly.

Diana opened her mouth to tell her sisters just what she thought of Berenford and then closed it again. She could not tell them the truth. Not Rebecca and Penelope, who would spread the tale until there was not a servant who did not know the truth. And servants gossiped with servants from other houses. No, she could not tell them. Nor could she tell Barbara, who would be certain to play some outrageous romp on Berenford in retaliation. Nor could she tell Annabelle, who waited eagerly for the news so that she could wed Lord Winsborough. Diana smiled. Barbara was accounted the actress in the family, but Diana would, this once, prove her equal.

"Berenford was quite a surprise," Diana said, evading their questions. "I had expected nothing like him. He is handsome, an excellent dancer, has the most extraordinary sense of humor, and a great deal of cleverness."

All of which was true, Diana reflected silently. Her sisters, however, were not so easily satisfied.

"Yes, but are you content to wed the man?" Barbara asked with no little exasperation.

Diana arched a delicate eyebrow. "Have I said I would cry off?" she retorted. "I am quite content with matters as they are."

Which was, again, the precise truth, though they were not to know the altered circumstances since last she had seen them. A cough at the doorway caused all five young women to turn and see Miss Tibbles standing in the doorway.

"I believe," the governess said severely, "that it is time to begin our lessons, girls."

"But we have just gotten to London!" Barbara protested angrily. "Even you cannot be so cruel as to make us go to work at once."

"Ah, but you are mistaken. I can," Miss Tibbles replied tranquilly. "We have been on the road two days and therefore have that much more work to catch up on. Lady Brisbane has put a parlor at our disposal, and you are to go there at once. A cold collation has been set out for us and once we have eaten, we will begin our work. Well, don't simply stare at me, go! I shall follow in a moment."

Reluctantly, the three youngest sisters filed out of the room, grumbling as they went. Annabelle continued to sit on the bed, and Miss Tibbles ignored her presence. Instead, she turned to Diana and said, approval patent in her voice, "That was well done, Lady Diana. Well done, indeed."

Then, with a brisk turn, Miss Tibbles whisked herself out of the room, leaving Diana and Annabelle to stare at one another in astonishment. Finally, unable to help themselves, they burst out laughing.

"Whatever did she mean?" Annabelle demanded when she had caught her breath.

Diana colored. "I must suppose she is pleased I have not drawn back from my betrothal," she said carelessly. It was evident, however, that Annabelle was not satisfied, and Diana hastened to give a new direction to her thoughts. "How is Miss Tibbles as a governess? She seems far too strict for the girls. Particularly Barbara."

Annabelle hesitated. "I will allow I thought so at first," she said slowly. "But now I begin to think Miss Tibbles will do very well with them."

"But she threatened to pour cold water over them as they slept!" Diana pointed out angrily.

"Yes, well, she has only had to do so once or twice," Annabelle replied. "I think, sometimes, she shares, or at any rate understands, their love of the outrageous."

"Miss Tibbles?" Diana gasped in disbelief.

Annabelle shifted uncomfortably. "Yes, well, the night she poured cold water over them, she made them change their shifts, put on wrappers, and trooped them downstairs where she made them something hot to drink and then proceeded to regale them with tales of some of the pranks she used to pull as a girl."

Diana stared at her sister, stunned at this unexpected portrait of Miss Tibbles. "Yes, but then how does she come to be a governess?" Diana protested at last. "And how do you know she told such tales? Perhaps Barbara and the twins were bamming you."

Now Annabelle flushed. "I went down and listened to Miss Tibbles as well," Annabelle admitted sheepishly.

"And that night Barbara did ask her why she became anything so stuffy as a governess."

"Well, what did she say?" Diana demanded impatiently when Annabelle hesitated again.

Annabelle sighed. "Miss Tibbles said that she became a governess to help prevent girls from making the mistakes she made."

"Stuff and nonsense!" Diana said roundly. "I think she enjoys browbeating the girls."

"And I think someone has too much time upon her hands," a voice said from the doorway.

Annabelle and Diana gasped and said, at the same moment, "Mama!"

Lady Westcott advanced into the room, a minatory look in her eyes. "I think you've both got too little to do," she repeated. "And you've lost your manners. Have the pair of you forgotten that the nuncheon my sister's cook has prepared is still waiting downstairs?"

Instantly, Diana was contrite. "I'm sorry, Mama," she said. "Is Aunt Ariana very vexed with us?"

Somewhat mollified, Lady Westcott shrugged and said, in a milder tone, "You know that my sister cannot stay angry with anyone for very long. Particularly not with her nieces. No, she is simply impatient for all of us to join her."

Lady Westcott turned to go, then paused. "Oh, by the by, Diana, Ariana thought it might be best, since your sisters have arrived, that you take Annabelle with you, as a sort of chaperone, when you go out driving with Berenford this afternoon."

And with that, Lady Westcott left the room, oblivious to the two girls, who stared at her retreating back with mouths gaping wide open.

Chapter Twelve

❧

Berenford climbed the steps of Lady Brisbane's town house in a more cheerful mood than he had the day before. By now the flowers ought to have arrived, and if he could not charm Diana today when he had her alone, he would be much astonished. And he would be, as he had promised her, the perfect gentleman. Behind him a groom held the reins of a pair of high-spirited, matched chestnuts. Berenford had chosen the pair, knowing just how much Diana would admire them.

The Duke of Berenford was naturally shown in at once to the drawing room. He started to step across the threshold of that room, then halted in astonishment. Instead of two ladies and Diana, he found Lord Westcott waiting for him as well and Diana nowhere to be seen.

Berenford took a deep breath and greeted the company. When he came to Lord Westcott, Berenford was relieved to see something of a twinkle in that gentleman's eyes. Aloud, however, Westcott issued a stern warning.

"My daughter informs me," Westcott said bluntly, "that she is not pleased with your recent masquerade. You'd best tread lightly, my boy, lightly indeed."

"I shall," Berenford replied fervently.

Behind him came a slight sound, and Berenford turned to see two young ladies dressed to go riding. Normally, he would have found the sight of Diana in her deep blue gown and matching pelisse entrancing. As it was, Berenford found his eyes drawn to the other young lady, dressed demurely in a pale pink gown and rose pelisse. There was a question in his eyes, and Lady Westcott hastened to answer it.

"May I present my second eldest daughter, Annabelle, Your Grace?" Lady Westcott said. "Annabelle, this is the Duke of Berenford, Diana's fiancé."

Diana held her breath. Would Annabelle recognize the groom, James, in Berenford? She had seen him only that once, in the entryway, but it was possible. And if she did, what would she say?

But Annabelle betrayed nothing. She politely greeted the Duke of Berenford and murmured all that was suitable in meeting him.

As for the man in question, Berenford felt himself bow, and he heard himself reply suitably, but still there was a question in his eyes, and, after a moment, Lady Westcott deigned to explain.

"We thought it best, Your Grace, that Annabelle accompany you and Diana on your drive this afternoon. We shouldn't wish anything to give rise to gossip," Lady Westcott said in a tranquil voice.

Again Berenford replied suitably and offered each lady an arm to escort them out to his carriage. There was no denying, however, that this was a blow to his plans. He had brought his high-perch phaeton, hoping to impress Diana with his driving skill and perhaps even causing her to lean against him for safety. But it would be cramped with the three of them, and Annabelle did not look the sort of girl to appreciate such a dangerous-looking vehicle.

In this Berenford was not mistaken. Annabelle took one look at the high-perch phaeton and almost drew back. Only the knowledge that if she did not accompany the pair, Mama would not allow Diana to go, kept her from doing so. After all, Annabelle told herself resolutely, Diana had accepted Berenford solely so that Annabelle could marry, and surely it was a far lesser sacrifice for her to swallow her fears and allow Berenford to hand her up into his phaeton.

Diana suppressed the laughter that threatened to bubble up from her throat at the look of temerity on Annabelle's face, the look of chagrin on Berenford's, and the stunned expression on the face of the groom. It was at this individual that Berenford allowed some of his exasperation to escape.

"You may as well wait here," Berenford told the luckless fellow. "The horses will have enough weight to pull as it is. I expect we shall be back shortly. Now stand away from their heads."

The fellow did as he was bid, and Berenford struggled to keep his high-spirited horses in check. Annabelle gripped Diana's arm tightly, her white face expressing clearly her thoughts upon the subject of such wild beasts and such precarious conveyances. Diana's cheeks, however, were flushed with excitement, and she made no effort to hide her approval as they moved swiftly down the street.

"What fine animals!" Diana exclaimed. "Where did you find them? Have you more like these in your stables? Will you let me try the reins?"

Berenford looked at Diana and took in her bright cheeks and shining eyes, and suddenly his good humor was restored. A quick look at her sister, however, and he said, answering her last question first, "Not today, I think. Your sister, I suspect, would not be equal to such excitement. These chestnuts are accustomed to no hand but mine, and I cannot answer for what they would do if you took the reins."

Annabelle shuddered, and Diana was quick to turn to her and say, "Don't worry, Belle. Berenford is remarkably skilled with horses. He won't let us overturn. And I promise I shan't take the reins today."

Annabelle smiled timidly at her sister. "I'm sorry to be such a ninny," she said to both Diana and Berenford.

"Nonsense," Berenford said gently. "You've merely a great deal of sense. Perhaps more than your sister and myself. But she is correct in saying I can bring us safely through the streets and the park."

Diana warmed at the consideration in Berenford's voice, and was pleased to feel Annabelle relax a trifle beside her. As though equally aware of the change in Annabelle, Berenford once more turned his attention to Diana.

"As for where I obtained these horses, they were bred on my own estate. I took part in their training," Berenford said with no little pride.

"Do you raise all your own horses?" Diana asked, transfixed by the notion.

Berenford shook his head. "No. We breed a few horses, but most I sell, and I have been known to obtain teams and individual horses at Tattersall's like anyone else."

Diana sighed at the name. "How I should like to go there," she said wistfully. "Papa says it is the one place in London where one might see the best and worst there is to be offered."

Beside her sister, Annabelle stirred in alarm. "Diana, you wouldn't?" she asked anxiously.

Diana flushed and frowned at her sister in warning.

Annabelle hastily swallowed whatever else she meant to say, and Diana risked a glance at Berenford. His attention was on the street, but before Diana could breathe a sigh of relief, he chuckled.

"I collect," he said dryly, "by your sister's words, that it would not be beyond you to attempt to enter Tattersall's? In masquerade perhaps?"

As this was so close to the mark, Annabelle grinned, and Diana found it hard to reply. "I . . . that was in my younger days, that is to say, I know it would not be the thing, at all," Diana stammered.

Berenford risked holding the reins in one hand and resting his other over hers for the briefest of moments. "It's all right," he said. "I shan't tell anyone." Then, in a lower more softly pitched voice he added, "I would take you to Tattersall's if I could, for I know you would love it above all things. But once we are married, I shall take you to my estate, and perhaps it will be of some consolation to see the stables my father and I have worked so hard to make among the finest in England."

Which was, Annabelle thought, an odd sort of romantic speech to make, but Diana seemed pleased enough by it. Certainly, she was looking at Berenford again as if she wanted nothing better than for him to kiss her.

Fortunately, for everyone's reputation, the park had been reached, and Berenford's attention was required to guide the horses, for it was the height of fashion to see and be seen at this hour here, and the drives were distinctly crowded. It seemed to Berenford that he could scarcely go ten feet without having to pull the horses up short to acknowledge the greeting of someone, either an acquaintance of his or of his mother's. Everyone, Berenford thought crossly, wanted to be introduced to the two young ladies at his side.

In this, Berenford was not mistaken. Within two minutes of his having entered the park, it seemed that everyone within that space knew that His Grace, the Duke of Berenford, was driving two young ladies, one of whom had fainted two nights ago at Almack's at the sight of him. And everyone did wish to see them together and be introduced to the girls. For everyone also wanted to know who the second young lady might be. And Berenford was therefore forced to smile amiably and grind his teeth silently as gentlemen requested permission to call upon Diana. Berenford took great pleasure in reminding them of his betrothal to her, but undeterred, they then asked if they might call upon her sister, Annabelle!

Perhaps the only person more distressed by all of this attention than Berenford was his sister-in-law to be. Annabelle did not know how to respond to the flattery, nor how to reply to the women who were patently jealous of her sister. Nor did Annabelle know how to answer the requests of the gentlemen to call upon her. She considered herself to be all but betrothed to Lord Winsborough, but that was a circumstance that could not be announced until after Diana was safely married. In the end, Annabelle turned a silent plea upon Berenford, and he nodded with a cold, determined smile. In moments he had turned the phaeton, and they were headed back toward Lady Brisbane's town house.

"Is everyone always so . . . so forward?" Annabelle asked timidly.

Berenford snorted. "Only when they sense a good *on-dit*," he said derisively.

There was, Diana thought, something in Berenford's

voice other than amused contempt. It was a hint of pain, and instinct told her it was directed at himself. This was not, however, the time to ask why. Instead, Diana tried to lighten his mood, and to that end she turned to her sister and said, "You must know, Annabelle, that we look hopelessly country missish! Of course everyone would wish to know who someone so elegant as His Grace, the Duke of Berenford, had condescended to be kind enough to escort in spite of that. And after I all but disgraced myself, fainting from the heat at Almack's, well, of course they came to look."

Diana ended with a slight shrug of her shoulder. Then she risked a glance at Berenford. His face was still set in grim lines, but a tiny hint of a smile began to tug at one corner of his mouth. He glanced at her and said severely, "Now you are bamming me, Lady Diana! No one could think that dress and pelisse came from any place save one of the most stylish modistes in London. And while your sister has not yet had an equal chance to replenish her wardrobe, surely it would be kinder, and more accurate, to guess that it was her prettiness which drew so many admiring eyes."

It might well be said that all three arrived back at Lady Brisbane's town house in perfect charity with one another. Berenford took his leave after saying all that was proper, though he did decline to come inside the house.

Diana and Annabelle went in alone. To Diana's surprise, Annabelle looked about, then drew her sister into the small parlor at the back of the house. There Annabelle stood, hands on hips and head tilted to one side as she said accusingly, "The Duke of Berenford looks very familiar, Diana. Indeed, if I didn't know it was impossible, I should say he looked exactly like one of the grooms on Papa's estate."

Diana checked that the parlor door was closed tightly. Then she drew Annabelle to a seat beside her and said, "You must swear not to tell a soul, Belle. Mama and Papa and Aunt Ariana know, of course, but no one else. Berenford did masquerade as a groom. When I saw him, here in London, I fainted dead away at the shock."

Annabelle looked at her sister in alarm. "But that is positively wicked! The pair of you would be ruined if anyone found out."

"That," Diana said dryly, "is precisely why I swore you to secrecy."

"But Diana, you cannot mean to marry a man who would do such a thing," Annabelle said in some agitation."

"What choice do I have?" Diana asked bitterly. "Mama, Papa, and Aunt Ariana all assure me I am ruined if I do not. Besides, if I do not marry Berenford, you cannot marry Winsborough."

That was a facer. Annabelle stared at her sister in unhappy silence. She sighed. "I suppose you are right," she said finally, "though I cannot like it. I wish you to be happy, Diana."

"Yes, well, I am not entirely dissatisfied with the match," Diana admitted.

"I still do not approve," Annabelle retorted. "What were Mama and Papa thinking of to choose him?"

Diana snorted. "You know very well what they were thinking of. They were thinking of Berenford's fortune and title and his good manners."

"Good manners?" Annabelle echoed incredulously.

Diana hesitated, then smiled. "Confess, Belle," she said. "You liked Berenford, didn't you? Didn't you find him all that was considerate and kind? Why he even refused to allow me to hold the reins, for fear it would distress you, and I did want most fervently to drive his cattle."

"That was probably due to consideration for his cattle rather than my feelings!" Annabelle retorted tartly. She hesitated, then added grudgingly, "I will allow, however, that today he seemed all that was proper."

"Well, then," Diana said with an assurance she did not feel, "all is well. Just please, please, do not tell Barbara or the twins the prank he pulled," she said fervently. "Heaven knows what they would do if they found out."

Annabelle shivered at the thought. "Rest assured," she replied, equally fervently. "I shan't tell them a word."

Chapter Thirteen

~

Diana was not, however, as sanguine about the match as she had tried to appear for Annabelle's sake. And when it came time to visit the Duchess of Berenford, she faced that ordeal with no little trepidation.

A mere formality, Lady Brisbane said airily. Nothing to worry about, Lady Westcott added. It would simply be a meeting to settle details of the wedding. After all, the match had been concocted with the approval, indeed the active efforts, of the Duchess of Berenford, so how could anything go wrong now?

As Diana stood in the Duchess of Berenford's drawing room on the appointed day, she realized bitterly that her aunt and mother had misjudged the matter. There was something about the way the Duchess of Berenford was regarding her that made Diana distinctly uneasy.

Behind Diana, both Lady Westcott and Lady Brisbane held their breath as they waited for the Duchess of Berenford to acknowledge her future daughter-in-law. In spite of their words of assurance to Diana, they knew only too well how unpredictable the Duchess of Berenford could be. When she finally did speak, it became evident that nothing was going to go as planned.

"So you're the hoyden who made a fool of herself at Almack's the other night," the Duchess of Berenford said spitefully. "I hope you've an explanation as to your disgraceful behavior?"

Diana had come intending to be all that was polite and demure. She had intended to do nothing to set up the Duchess of Berenford's back. Now, however, Diana tilted her chin militantly and took a step forward. She curtsied to the duchess and said, her voice cool and steady, "Good afternoon, Your Grace. I am happy to meet you at last."

The Duchess of Berenford thumped her cane upon the floor. "Don't try to flummery me, girl!" she said with narrowed eyes. "I know you've more wit than hair, or I wouldn't have chosen you for my son. Answer my question."

Diana's own eyes narrowed, briefly, In a way that would have alarmed Lady Westcott had she been standing where she could see her daughter's face. Diana smiled sweetly and said, "Thank you, I will take a seat."

As her aunt and mother and future mother-in-law all gasped at such defiant behavior, Diana settled on a sofa and regarded the Duchess of Berenford with wide, clear eyes as she continued, "Almack's? Several nights ago? Why I believe I fainted from the heat. Or was it my hem? Yes, I believe it was my hem. The toe of my shoe caught in the hem, and I tripped. Clumsy of me, I'll allow, but my maid has orders to shorten my hems, just a trifle, and I cannot think that it will happen again."

Lady Brisbane winced. Lady Westcott closed her eyes and murmured a prayer toward the ceiling. Diana held her breath. For what seemed an eternity, the Duchess of Berenford stared at Diana, and then slowly she set aside her cane and began to clap her hands.

Lady Westcott's eyes flew open. Diana and Lady Brisbane stared at the duchess as though she had gone mad, an impression compounded when the woman said, "Bravo!"

The Duchess of Berenford paused. She eyed each of her guests in turn shrewdly, then she said haughtily, "A duchess never apologizes." To Diana she added, "You've a quick mind, and I approve of that. Nor do I think you'll bore my son. I don't particularly like you, but that's neither here nor there. All that matters is that you be a proper wife to my son and show me the respect I am due. In return, I shall endeavor not to chafe at you more than is absolutely necessary. Which will," she added with a small smile, "no doubt be more than you will like."

All sorts of tart words hovered on the tip of Diana's tongue, and her mother hastened to speak before any of them could escape. "You are very kind, Your Grace," Lady Westcott said to the duchess. "I am certain Diana is conscious of the favor you are conferring on her."

Lady Brisbane knew better than her sister how to address the Duchess of Berenford. She stepped forward and took a seat on the sofa opposite Diana. Then, with a bluntness that matched the other woman's own, she said, "Well, were we not right to pair up your son and my niece?"

The Duchess of Berenford shrugged. "We shall see. I still am not entirely satisfied. Tell me, my girl," she said, addressing Diana again, "you do not mean to be missish about my son's mistresses, do you?"

At Lady Westcott's gasp of outrage, the duchess turned to her and snapped, "Oh, do sit down and stop being a ninny! I asked your daughter a perfectly sensible question. My son is a man, and men have mistresses. I want to be certain your daughter is not going to enact him any Cheltenham tragedies when she discovers that fact."

"I assure you," Diana said through gritted teeth, "I do not engage in tragedies."

The Duchess of Berenford smiled in satisfaction. "Good. Then you will allow him to go his way without hindrance?"

In a deceptively sweet voice Diana countered with a question of her own. "Do you think, Your Grace, that Berenford will allow me to go my way without hindrance? To have my own ciscisbeos?"

The Duchess of Berenford sniffed. "Certainly," she said coolly. "My son is a sensible man. Naturally, you must remain entirely faithful until you have presented him with an heir. Preferably until there is a second son, as well, just in case anything should happen to the eldest, you understand. After that, well, I am certain Jeremy could have no objection, so long as you are discreet."

"On the contrary," an angry voice said from the doorway of the room, "Jeremy will have every objection should Diana attempt to play him false!"

The Duchess of Berenford was not perturbed. "Come in, Jeremy, and greet your fiancée. It is extremely rude to stand there listening and not make your presence known."

Berenford came forward, his face still set in angry lines. He inclined his head toward his mother as he said, "I thought I was making my presence known." He turned toward Diana and added, "I meant what I said."

Lady Brisbane and Lady Westcott looked at one another helplessly. The Duchess of Berenford pressed her lips together in patent disapproval. The Duchess of Berenford stared down at Diana, waiting for her reply. Only Diana seemed unperturbed. Without haste she smoothed her skirt, straightened her shoulders, and looked up at Berenford with an apparently tranquil expression.

Inwardly, however, Diana seethed. Must he make things

even more awkward than they already were? And did he mean to keep a mistress even as he demanded fidelity from her? Diana wondered miserably.

Whether she was angrier at the Duchess of Berenford or her son, Diana was uncertain. She knew only that she devoutly wished to rattle the pair of them. So now Diana smiled and said sweetly. "I shall no doubt be as faithful a wife as you are a husband, Your Grace."

"Don't be impertinent, child!" the duchess snapped out with a thump of her cane.

Berenford, however, smiled thinly. "Then you will no doubt live a very dull life," he replied.

Diana stared up at Berenford, wondering if she had heard, had understood correctly what he said, hoping that she had. As though oblivious to everyone else, Berenford slowly sat down beside her and possessed himself of Diana's hand. He kissed her fingertips.

The warmth in Berenford's eyes as he regarded Diana caused her color to rise. Sweet Lord, could it be possible that he felt toward her as she felt toward him? Diana wondered in astonishment. That he meant all the loverlike things he said? Hope rose in Diana's breast.

"Very prettily said," Lady Brisbane said approvingly.

"Very prettily done," Lady Westcott added with a smile.

"Fustian!" the Duchess of Berenford said with a snort of disgust. "Jeremy, you must begin as you mean to go on, and if you do not intend to live under the cat's paw, you had best make clear to the girl that you will tolerate no disrespect. I chose her precisely so you would not need to indulge in this sort of romantic nonsense. If you begin to do so now, she will no doubt expect it for the rest of your married lives. Diana, my son will do as he wishes, and you will behave as your position requires. Have I made myself clear?"

Now Berenford turned to his mother and dropped a kiss on her forehead. "You have made yourself eminently clear, Mama," he said in a weary voice. "And your guests have undoubtedly made you tired. I shall escort them out. Ladies? I am certain you will see my mother another day."

"But we have not yet discussed the wedding," the duchess protested.

"You can do so another day," Berenford replied coolly.

Then, ignoring his mother's gasp of outrage, Berenford shepherded the three ladies from the room. Lady Brisbane and Lady Westcott murmured suitable farewells, but did not greatly protest. They were far too concerned what sort of outburst Diana might indulge in if allowed to remain. Uppermost in their minds was the need to remove her to a safe distance from the duchess before something was said that shattered the betrothal altogether.

As for Diana, she allowed herself to be guided from the room. There would be time enough later for the inevitable battle between the Duchess of Berenford and herself, if she married James/Jeremy.

When they reached the street, Diana watched Berenford hand her mother and aunt into the waiting carriage. When he turned to her, Diana grasped the moment to say, urgently, but with her voice pitched low, "We must speak about this, Berenford. I meant what I said inside. I will not be complacent if you take a mistress."

Berenford regarded Diana steadily. His voice was grave as he replied, "I, too, meant what I said. I mean to be a faithful husband and shall expect the same of you."

Before Diana could find the words to reply to this very gratifying speech, Berenford kissed her cheek. A warm glow swept through Diana. Both cheeks turned a bright red as Berenford smiled down at her.

"By the by," he said, "I do think you might call me Jeremy."

"Jeremy." Diana echoed the word in a voice that was scarcely above a whisper.

Berenford nodded. "You'd best get into the carriage," he said. "Your mother and aunt are waiting."

Diana went, her mind a whirl of emotions and tangled thoughts.

Berenford watched until the carriage was out of sight, and then he turned and mounted the steps. He intended to have a discussion with his mother that would settle, once and for all, the limits to her meddling.

But the duchess was well aware she had offended her son, and she was waiting, on her guard. The moment he stepped into the drawing room, she took the offensive.

"Well," the Duchess of Berenford said in her most regal voice, "that was quite a display of temper, Jeremy, and I must say, I am most disappointed in you!"

Berenford advanced into the room, determined to press his own attack. "Now look here, Mother," he said. "You are to treat my wife with far greater respect than you did today or I'll banish you to the dower house."

The Duchess of Berenford laughed. "You wouldn't dare," she said contemptuously. "You, of all people, know how wicked my tongue is when I'm enraged, and I would be enraged if you banished me."

"I won't be blackmailed," he retorted calmly. "Nor will I have you set out to ruin my marriage before it has even begun. Is that clear?"

The duchess sniffed. "What is quite clear to me is that you mean to be a tyrant as your father was when we first married. Well, I will not have it. I would not tolerate it from him, and I certainly will not tolerate it from you, Jeremy."

Berenford smiled grimly. "No, but you counsel my future wife to tolerate such treatment, or did I misunderstand what you told her?"

The duchess shrugged. "That is entirely different. You are my son. Naturally, I should prefer that you, and not she, should have the upper hand in your marriage."

"Nevertheless," Berenford said in a dangerously quiet voice, "you will give over your attempts to mold Diana. I shall manage my marriage as I see fit."

"Very well," the Duchess of Berenford said with a sigh. "It is your affair, after all."

"How delighted I am that you are finally able to grasp that simple fact," Berenford said with irony.

Now the duchess stared at her son with narrowed eyes. There was more than a hint of asperity in her voice as she said sharply, "If you didn't want me to meddle in your marriage, then why didn't you choose a wife, yourself, years ago?"

"I did, or have you forgotten?" he retorted.

"I don't mean Clarissa. You were far too green a boy then. That was an unmitigated disaster. But you have had plenty of time, since, to look about you for a better choice," the duchess snapped back.

Berenford stared off into the distance for a long moment before he answered his mother. "Perhaps," he said softly, "I was waiting for someone precisely like Diana."

Before the duchess could respond to that outrageous pronouncement, the drawing room doors were flung open, and a petite lady appeared.

"Aunt Elizabeth!" Berenford said with a crow of delight. "What are you doing here?"

As he went forward to greet her, Berenford's mother narrowed her eyes. "Yes, Elizabeth, what are you doing here?" she asked suspiciously.

The newcomer smiled at the Duchess of Berenford. "Why, I've come to discover everything I can about Jeremy's bride-to-be, of course," she said, unabashed as she hugged her nephew. Still, there was an anxious look in her eyes as she peered up at him and asked, "Are you happy, Jeremy? Will she do?"

Some part of Berenford seemed to immediately withdraw from his aunt. Behind him, the duchess said impatiently, "Of course Lady Diana will do! I chose her most carefully for Jeremy. He needs to breed an heir, and her family is certainly fertile. There are five children. All girls to be sure, but no doubt Jeremy will manage matters somewhat better. In any event, outside of a slight tendency to impertinence, I think Lady Diana will do very well. She already has the necessary hauteur for a duchess."

"Does she," Elizabeth said thoughtfully, drawing off her gloves. "That does not sound very promising. I suppose I shall simply have to see for myself."

"No!" Both Jeremy and his mother said the word at the same moment.

Aunt Elizabeth tilted her head to one side and considered. "I think, yes, I think you had better tell me all about your betrothed, Jeremy," she said. "And then I mean to do precisely as I think best."

"As you always have," the duchess grumbled wearily.

Berenford looked from his mother to his aunt. He could not speak entirely freely, but he would do his best to persuade Aunt Elizabeth that Diana was an unexceptionable

choice. Otherwise she was, he knew grimly, perfectly capable of trying to thrust a spoke in the wheels and prevent the
marriage. And, dearly as he loved her, that Jeremy was not
góing to allow his aunt to do.

Chapter Fourteen

⁓

The small, shabbily dressed woman paused as she stepped down from the carriage. "Are you certain?" she asked the coachman.

"It's Lady Brisbane's house, all right," the coachman confirmed.

"Thank you. Wait for me. I shan't be long," the woman said firmly.

She took a deep breath and then began to climb the steps. Nothing in her face or bearing betrayed the concern she felt. Instead, her bearing was erect, her expression calm as she rapped at the knocker on Lady Brisbane's door. When it opened, the footman stared at the woman in disdain. "The servants' entrance is in the back," he said haughtily.

The woman raised her eyebrows. Her voice was more haughty as she answered, "I am here to see Lady Diana. Please tell her that Mrs. Cathcart wishes to see her."

Had Lady Brisbane's majordomo not appeared at that moment, the footman would have committed a horrible solecism. As it was, the majordomo instantly recognized the quality of the visitor, despite her shabby attire. He also recognized the crest on the carriage standing outside waiting for her.

Elbowing the poor footman aside, Lady Brisbane's majordomo bowed deeply and said, "Please come this way, Mrs. Cathcart. I shall tell Lady Diana you are here. It is, perhaps, a trifle early for callers, but I collect your need to speak with her is urgent?"

"Most urgent," Mrs. Cathcart confirmed.

The majordomo showed Mrs. Cathcart into a small parlor at the back of the house. "You will be more private here," he said, anxious to explain that he meant no offense. "Lady Brisbane and Lady Westcott are already occupying the drawing room."

Now Mrs. Cathcart regarded the majordomo shrewdly. "You are a wise fellow, aren't you?" she said. "I thank you for your perception and your discretion."

The majordomo bowed again and permitted himself a small smile as he withdrew from the room to summon Lady Diana. As for the poor footman, he would receive a lecture later in the servants' quarters as to the necessity of sizing up one's callers by far more than the cost of their clothing. Whoever Mrs. Cathcart was, she was most certainly Quality.

Diana, summoned downstairs by a cryptic message, entered the parlor warily. She paused on the threshold and regarded the petite woman staring out the window carefully. There was something about her that seemed very familiar.

"Mrs. Cathcart?" Diana asked stiffly.

The woman turned and stared straight at Diana, appraising her. The gaze was not a friendly one.

"Lady Diana?" Diana nodded, and Mrs. Cathcart went on coolly, "you may wish to close the door, Lady Diana, so that we may be more private. I do not think you will wish anyone to overhear us."

Diana did so. Then she moved closer. Who was this woman? And what did she want?

Mrs. Cathcart allowed the scrutiny. She wished, after all, to make an appraisal of her own. Her shrewd eyes took in Diana's curling blond hair, the blue eyes, the moderate height, and neatly trim figure. "So you are the young woman who is to marry Jeremy," she said.

There was no welcome in her voice. Diana was puzzled. "The Duke of Berenford and I are betrothed," she agreed stiffly.

"Why?"

One word, spoken curtly, implacably. It roused Diana's anger. "Why not?" she countered. "It is a suitable, indeed a sensible, match."

Mrs. Cathcart snorted in a most unladylike way. "Suitable! Sensible!" she said derisively. "And do you wish for nothing more than that?"

Slowly, Diana sat down. She studied Mrs. Cathcart for a long moment before she said, "I do not wish to be rude, but who are you, Mrs. Cathcart, to ask me such things?"

For a long moment the woman stared at Diana, and then a smile crept grudgingly onto her lips. She nodded, "Yes, I suppose you have a right to ask that of me. Has Jeremy never mentioned my name?"

Diana shook her head. Mrs. Cathcart tilted her head to one side. "That is a telling point," she said, "and not in your favor."

Once more Diana's temper erupted into anger. "By what right do you judge such things?" she demanded. "Jeremy and I have given our consent to the match and so have our families. By what right do you question our betrothal now?"

"By the right of love," Mrs. Cathcart answered softly. "And I do love Jeremy very much, you see."

Diana's face went white. The room seemed to spin about

her. Surely, the woman before her was too old for Jeremy? Surely, she could not mean what she seemed to mean?

"And does he love you?" Diana heard herself ask in a hard, grim voice.

"I have reason to think so," Mrs. Cathcart said complacently.

Diana rose to her feet and began to pace about the small room. It was impossible! Unbelievable! A horrible jest of fate!

"How dare you confront me here?" Diana demanded.

For a moment Mrs. Cathcart stared at Diana as if the girl had lost her wits. Then, slowly, comprehension dawned upon her, and she laughed.

"I believe," Mrs. Cathcart said with gentle amusement, "that you are under some sort of misapprehension. Did you think I meant I was Jeremy's mistress?"

Diana flushed. "I . . . I don't know what you mean," she stammered.

Mrs. Cathcart's smile broadened. "Oh, dear, we have begun badly. I should have explained at the outset. I am Jeremy's aunt, his mother's sister, you see. And I must say that I am immensely flattered that any other possibility could even have occurred to you."

But Diana scarcely heard these last words. She stared at Mrs. Cathcart. "You are Jeremy's aunt?" she echoed. "But your clothes! I mean . . ." she began to apologize as she realized how rude her outburst must sound.

Mrs. Cathcart laughed. "Yes, I know. It is the despair of my sister, and all the rest of my family, for that matter. I am the one who is in disgrace, you know. I married beneath myself—a mere country vicar. Worse, I refuse to be addressed as Lady Elizabeth."

Mrs. Cathcart paused and looked down at her dress. Her

eyes twinkled merrily as she went on, "We haven't a great deal of money, and somehow it has never seemed important that I have or wear the latest fashions. I married for love, you see, and have never regretted it. Which is perhaps what my sister finds hardest to forgive. I am disappointed, however, that Jeremy never saw fit to mention me."

Mrs. Cathcart paused again. She tilted her head to one side and said, "I love Jeremy dearly, and heretofore he has always confided in me. But he has not come to see me since his betrothal to you was announced. And when I spoke with him yesterday, there was far too much constraint in his voice. Oh, he said all that was proper, of course, and sang your praises quite prettily. But I know that my sister pressed Jeremy into the match, and I wanted to see for myself the woman he has chosen to marry. Particularly because I have heard some alarming tales since you arrived in London. A contretemps at Almack's, I believe?"

Diana did not at once reply. How could she without revealing what had occurred back home? Had Jeremy told his aunt about the masquerade? If not, how was she to explain her behavior without betraying them both?

Mrs. Cathcart watched the mixture of emotions that crossed Diana's face. When the girl did not answer, she sighed. "I know my sister very well," she said quietly. "Having once gotten Jeremy to agree to the match, she would never allow him to draw back, and he is too much the gentleman to admit misgivings to anyone, including me. But I thought that seeing you would tell me what sort of match it was. I see it is worse than I thought."

"No!" Diana instinctively cried out.

"No?" Mrs. Cathcart echoed. "Then tell me how it is."

"To what purpose?" Diana asked warily.

"So that I may decide whether to take a hand and end

this match if I think it unsuitable," Mrs. Cathcart answered bluntly.

"Oh, it is eminently suitable," Diana said, a trifle bitterly as she emphasized the last word.

Mrs. Cathcart smiled thinly. "Perhaps 'unsuitable' is not the best word for what I meant," she agreed. "Let us say rather that I wish Jeremy to be happy. If I think you and he will not be, if I believe this to be a truly loveless match, I shall do my best to persuade Jeremy to cry off."

"Even though it would ruin both of us?" Diana asked, a speculative gleam in her eye.

Mrs. Cathcart stared unblinkingly at Diana. Her voice was soft and earnest as she said, "I was said to be ruined when I married Mr. Cathcart. But these have been the happiest years of my life. I should like to see the same for Jeremy. What use is one's social position if one is forced to a lifetime of unhappiness with someone else? Such a loveless match might have suited my sister, right down to the ground, but it would never suit Jeremy. He has too much life, too much passion in him, to be happy that way."

Diana looked at her hands. She heard the passion in Mrs. Cathcart's own voice, the concern for Jeremy that had been absent when the Duchess of Berenford spoke of her son. And she knew that Mrs. Cathcart was speaking the truth.

Quietly, her hands gripped tightly together, Diana said, "Will you tell me about Jeremy?" When Mrs. Cathcart did not at once answer, Diana rushed to add, "I know so little about him, you see."

Slowly, Mrs. Cathcart sat down. She regarded Diana steadily and even drummed her fingers on the arm of the chair. "You do care about my nephew, then?" she asked.

Diana lifted her eyes to meet Mrs. Cathcart's stern gaze.

"I think I do," she said simply, "but I have known Jeremy too short a time to be sure."

Mrs. Cathcart nodded. "Sensible," she said approvingly. "Before I answer your question, however, I should like you to answer mine. I have spoken with Jeremy, of course, but I should like to hear how you perceive what has passed between the pair of you. I should particularly like to know the tale behind your behavior at Almack's."

Diana hesitated. So Jeremy had not told her about the masquerade. How was she to explain what had occurred at Almack's without speaking about that?

As Diana hesitated, Mrs. Cathcart prodded her. "Start at the beginning, my dear," she suggested gently.

"The betrothal was arranged by my parents," Diana said quietly, "and by Jeremy's mother. My aunt had a hand in it as well," she added dryly.

"And why did you agree?" Mrs. Cathcart asked, a pinched look of disapproval on her lips.

Diana sighed and looked away, then back again. "Because my parents wanted me to wed. Because I am the eldest, and my next younger sister wants to marry. Because, oh, because I thought I would never find anyone to care about so what difference did it make whom I wed?"

Mrs. Cathcart nodded slowly. "Jeremy said much the same," she said. "And do you still feel that way? Has he roused no warmer feelings in you, yet?" she asked shrewdly.

Diana flushed. "Some," she admitted, wary. "More than I am certain is wise."

To her surprise, Mrs. Cathcart nodded approvingly. "That is the most encouraging thing you have told me yet," she said warmly. "But then why the contretemps at Almack's, my dear?"

There was no help for it. Diana threw caution to the winds and told Mrs. Cathcart, a little at any rate, about Jeremy's masquerade and her response when she saw him at Almack's.

Mrs. Cathcart seemed to understand perfectly. "Yes, I see," she said when Diana had finished. "It would not have been easy for you, and my nephew would not have understood until you told him. How much easier it is for men, my dear, than for ourselves. Still," Mrs. Cathcart said with twinkling eyes, "that masquerade is a memory you and Jeremy will share and jest about for the rest of your lives."

Before Diana could answer, the parlor door was thrown open, and both ladies turned to see why. Lady Brisbane stood in the doorway, with Lady Westcott at her back. Both of them stared at Diana and Mrs. Cathcart in astonishment.

"Diana, what is going on?" Lady Westcott asked her daughter carefully.

Diana rose to her feet. "Mama, Aunt Ariana, this is Mrs. Cathcart, Lord Berenford's aunt. Mrs. Cathcart, may I present my mother, Lady Westcott, and my aunt, Lady Brisbane."

Startled, the two sisters peered closely at the shabbily dressed woman before them. "Elizabeth?" Lady Brisbane asked uncertainly.

"Have I changed so very much, Ariana?" Mrs. Cathcart asked softly.

Both Lady Westcott and Lady Brisbane rushed forward and hugged Mrs. Cathcart. It was an awkward tangle of arms and tears and laughter and mumbled words. Diana watched in bewilderment. Finally, Lady Westcott turned to her daughter and said, in explanation, "Ariana and Elizabeth and I were the dearest of bosom bows when we were girls. Then Elizabeth married Mr. Cathcart, and we were forbidden to go and see her. It's been over twenty years since we last did so."

"But you married a vicar!" Diana blurted out before she could stop herself.

"Precisely," Mrs. Cathcart said with a twinkle in her eyes. "As I told you, I married beneath myself—at least in the eyes of my family and the *ton*."

It was Lady Brisbane, however, who turned to Diana and added, "Our parents were afraid that Elizabeth's example might corrupt us. We were told she had disgraced herself, and we were forbidden to even think of her." Lady Brisbane paused, turned to Mrs. Cathcart, and added softly, "But naturally we did so, anyway."

More hugs and laughter then, and hastily uttered explanations meant to span twenty years of absence among three friends. Finally, the words drifted to an end, and all four women were seated.

"I still don't understand, Elizabeth," Lady Westcott said slowly, "why you were in here speaking to Diana. The footman said you never even asked for us."

Mrs. Cathcart hesitated. Her eyes were suspiciously moist as she replied. "I didn't know if either of you would want to see me. Especially after all this time. You never answered my letters after all."

Lady Westcott and Lady Brisbane looked at one another.

"Papa!"

"He must have intercepted the letters!"

"Oh, if he were only still alive, I should tell him what I think of that!"

"Elizabeth, we never got your letters," Lady Westcott explained. "If we had, of course we would have written."

"I did try to," Lady Brisbane added darkly. "Papa must

have found out and gotten my letters from my maid. If she were still in my service, I should dismiss her at once."

"Well, at any rate, I have found you again," Mrs. Cathcart said mistily.

"Yes, but why were you speaking to Diana?" Lady Westcott asked, returning to her original question.

Mrs. Cathcart quirked an eyebrow. "Have you forgotten, Delwinia? The Duke of Berenford is my nephew. I got wind of this most extraordinary betrothal and thought I would come to see for myself precisely what sort of girl Jeremy had gotten himself betrothed to. And why."

Lady Westcott looked nervously at her hands. "I don't know why you call it extraordinary," she said defensively. "It is a most suitable match."

"Suitable?" Mrs. Cathcart echoed derisively. "I do not question that the *ton* will think so. But it seems to me that my sister said that Jeremy and Diana had never met before the betrothal was announced. Now I call that very extraordinary, don't you?"

"It has been done before," Lady Brisbane retorted sharply. "Your sister and I discussed every aspect of such an arrangement before we presented the matter to Diana and Jeremy, I assure you. Your sister agreed that it would be a sensible match."

"She would," Mrs. Cathcart said with a distinctly unladylike snort. "Well, I don't care a fig for what she thinks. It is my nephew's future that is at stake. And Diana's. That is what concerns me now. I came to see whether this match was as bloodless as I had heard and, if so, I meant to do whatever I could to stop it."

For several long moments Lady Westcott and Lady Brisbane stared at Mrs. Cathcart. "Well?" Lady Westcott said when she could stand it no longer. "Do you mean to oppose the match? To thrust a spoke in the wheels?"

Mrs. Cathcart looked at Diana, hesitated, then smiled. She held out a hand to the girl and Diana took it. "No, I shan't intervene," Mrs. Cathcart said gently. "What began poorly may turn out well, after all. Though I shan't," she added sternly, "hesitate to do so if I learn anything that proves me wrong."

"You couldn't, wouldn't do something that might ruin both my niece and your nephew?" Lady Brisbane asked anxiously.

Mrs. Cathcart raised her eyebrows. She gave them the same answer she had given Diana. "Do you truly think, Ariana, knowing the decision I made more than twenty years ago, and knowing that I do not, for one moment, regret it, that I would choose respectability over happiness for Jeremy?"

As Lady Westcott and Lady Brisbane watched in dismay, Mrs. Cathcart turned to Diana and said, "I must be going. Will you walk me to my carriage, Diana?"

"Of course."

Lady Westcott and Lady Brisbane would have followed, but a warning glance from Mrs. Cathcart stopped them. They could only hope Diana would have the sense to continue to charm Elizabeth. Heaven knew what disaster their friend would cause otherwise.

They need not have worried. Diana and Jeremy's aunt talked companionably about London as the now chastened footman fetched Mrs. Cathcart's things. A few moments later, Diana was standing outside Lady Brisbane's town house with Mrs. Cathcart. She stared in surprise at the elegant equipage waiting at the curb.

"My sister said that she did not wish to be disgraced by

having me seen driving about town in a hired hack," Mrs. Cathcart observed with some amusement. "She insisted most strenuously that I borrow her carriage. I almost said that people would wonder at her lending it to someone as shabbily dressed as I, but thought better of it. I just know she would have insisted on refurbishing my wardrobe if I did so."

Mrs. Cathcart's eyes invited Diana to smile along with her at the joke, and Diana did so. She couldn't help liking Jeremy's aunt—particularly when Mrs. Cathcart thanked by name the coachman who helped her into the carriage.

"I am leaving London this afternoon," Mrs. Cathcart said earnestly to Diana as she settled her skirts about her. "But if ever you should wish to talk again, about Jeremy and marriage, please come and see me. I think it will do, but I should not wish to see either you or Jeremy made unhappy by a mistake that cannot be undone once the knot is tied."

"I shall," Diana promised and listened carefully as Mrs. Cathcart gave her the direction of her husband's country vicarage.

"It can be reached in a couple of hours," Mrs. Cathcart assured her. "And remember, I shall always be happy to see you there."

"Will I see you at the wedding?" Diana asked.

Mrs. Cathcart smiled. "Of course. But I warn you," she added sternly, "that even at the last moment I shall not hesitate to raise my voice to prevent the marriage, should I think it a mistake."

Diana nodded. The coachman closed the door and climbed into the box. Diana watched until the carriage had reached the end of the street and turned out of sight. What an extraordinary woman! Diana thought. She turned to go inside. No doubt her mother and Aunt Ariana would be waiting to pounce on her. She did not relish the notion, but there was no avoiding it, Diana knew, and she preferred to deal with unpleasantness rather than delaying it.

Chapter Fifteen

❧

Inside, Lady Brisbane and Lady Westcott were indeed waiting to pounce on Diana.

"You must not let Elizabeth overset you," Lady Brisbane said sternly. "I am very fond of her, but she has always had the oddest notions."

"Yes, and fond as she is of Berenford, she cannot know as well as his own mother what is best for him," Lady Westcott added.

That drew a glare from her sister, but Diana only smiled wearily and told them both, "Mrs. Cathcart has said she will not oppose the match, so you need not worry. And I am glad to have met her."

Lady Brisbane and her sister looked at one another. Lady Brisbane cleared her throat. "Yes, well, that is excellent. I am pleased to hear it."

Clearly, however, her fears had not entirely been set to rest. She might have said more, but a knock sounded at the parlor door, and a moment later, Lady Brisbane's major-domo opened it.

"My lady," he said to Lady Westcott, "there is a caller, and I think you had best come and see him."

Puzzled, Lady Westcott immediately moved toward the

door. Diana would have followed, but Lady Brisbane put out a hand to stop her.

"Whoever it is does not concern us," Lady Brisbane said softly, "and I have wanted to speak with you alone, anyway, since yesterday when we saw Berenford's mother. I collect you think she was appalling, but you must know that when one is a duchess, one can get away with indulging in such eccentric speech."

"Indeed?" Diana asked, a speculative gleam in her eyes now.

Lady Brisbane regarded her niece shrewdly. "When one is an *elderly* duchess, I should have said. You, Diana, will not have such freedom. You will have to guard your tongue until you are at least your mother's age."

Diana sniffed decisively, but Lady Brisbane pressed hastily on. "Never mind that. What I really wished to speak to you about is being Berenford's wife. His mother was entirely wrong.

"Oh?" Diana asked warily.

Lady Brisbane proceeded as if she had not heard. "This business of mistresses, for example. Naturally, you will tell Berenford you object if he is so foolish or so indiscreet as to allow you to discover he is keeping one. Secondly, even after you present Berenford with an heir, even after two, you would be wisest not to take a lover. Instead, you will be wisest to make Berenford your lover."

Lady Brisbane paused and smiled with secret satisfaction. Then she went on, "I don't mean to shock you, my dear Diana, but it is important that someone speak bluntly to you about these things. And dearly though I love my sister, your mother, she has the oddest notions about the marriage bed. One would think she found it distinctly unpleasant! Well, you are her daughter, so I suppose it is possible you will as well, but I must say, I hope you will not. It is possible to derive a great deal of pleasure therein."

Again Lady Brisbane paused. Diana blushed. Her hand crept up to her cheek as she remembered how it felt when James, when Berenford, kissed her. How the warmth seemed to spread through her like fire and how she wanted more. She didn't answer Lady Brisbane. How could she? What could she say? That there was no need to worry because her nature was as wanton as it was possible to be? No, Diana didn't dare say a word.

Still, Lady Brisbane seemed satisfied, for after a moment she went on. "Now where was I? Oh, yes. After you've presented Berenford with his heirs, Diana, rather than look around for a lover, you would do far better to bring Berenford to your bed as often as possible. He is said to be a skilled lover, and once you have succeeded in convincing him that he need not treat you as if you were a fragile porcelain doll, well, you may find a great deal of satisfaction in his lovemaking."

Lady Brisbane paused and frowned. "Unfortunately, it may take some persuading for him to believe that. Berenford will no doubt have been brought up to believe that he must treat you with a certain degree of respect, in the bedroom as well as without. And if you do need to persuade him, it is best done after you present Berenford with his heir. Otherwise, he may wonder who taught you to think of such a thing. That is how I handled Lord Brisbane, and it worked like a charm."

The image of Lady Brisbane and the late Lord Brisbane in the bedroom, with her trying to persuade his lordship to love her, was enough to make Diana blink several times. She wanted to ask what advice her aunt would give her son upon his marriage, but she didn't quite dare.

"Well?" Lady Brisbane said impatiently. "Have you heard a word I've said?"

Diana looked at her aunt and her lips twitched as she replied, "I do not think you need to worry that Berenford will treat me with an excessive degree of respect."

Alarmed, Lady Brisbane demanded, "What do you mean? What has he done? Why should you say such a thing?"

Impossible to answer honestly. Impossible to tell Aunt Ariana that Berenford had shown no reluctance to hold her and kiss her or treat her as he would his mistress. Impossible to tell her it would not be necessary to wait until after an heir or two was born to persuade Berenford that Diana would not find lovemaking disagreeable. And yet, Berenford had promised to act the perfect gentleman, at least until she requested him to do otherwise, Diana remembered uneasily. Had he meant it? There had been no chance to tell yesterday, for Annabelle had been with them, and the park far too public a place for any affectionate displays. Would it have been different had they been alone?

Abruptly, Diana realized she had to say something. It was evident from Aunt Ariana's expression that she was growing genuinely alarmed. Desperately, Diana cast about for something safe to reply.

"Well, that is to say, I did not think gentlemen generally regarded their brides so warmly. Or were so quick to kiss their hands. Mama said . . ."

Diana allowed her voice to trail off. She kept her eyes demurely on the floor and her hands neatly folded in her lap. Out of the corner of her eye she did risk a glance at her aunt and was relieved at what she saw.

Lady Brisbane snorted. "Your mother! All sorts of odd notions she has! How I ever ended up with such a prude of a sister, I'll never know. She told you, I'll be bound, that a gentleman never touches a girl, except to dance or hand her up into a carriage, until after they are married. Am I right?" Diana nodded, and Lady Brisbane snorted again. "Ridiculous! Many a gentleman allows himself a slightly warmer gesture than that. They think girls like it, and, what's more, they are right!" She leaned forward and patted Diana's hand. "There, we've nothing to worry about after all. Still, such kind gestures do not mean that after marriage Berenford will continue them or that he will understand how warmly you might welcome him to your bed. That is something you will still need to show him. But after you've presented him with his heirs," she warned.

Diana blushed, and Lady Brisbane counted it a good thing. Her sister, Delwinia, might be a fool, but there was no denying that it was better for a gentleman to be certain his bride came to him an innocent, than for him to have doubts. There would be plenty of time to counsel Diana how to begin to woo Berenford after they had been married a while. All in all, Lady Brisbane considered the interview with Diana to have been a success, and she suggested Diana run along and join her sisters.

Lady Brisbane had no notion the turmoil she had roused in her poor niece's breast! Nor did it help Diana to discover that Lord Winsborough was in the drawing room with her mother and Annabelle.

Diana hesitated on the threshold of the room. It was not that she disliked Winsborough; it was that her own thoughts were in such a turmoil, and she had no desire to see anyone just now. She cursed herself for forgetting that it was a caller who had drawn her mother out of the parlor. Still, there was no escape; she had been seen and must come forward to greet Lord Winsborough. She smiled.

"Ah, Diana, there you are. Lord Winsborough, I am sure you remember my eldest daughter?" Lady Westcott said graciously.

Winsborough inclined his head. "Lady Diana, it is good to see you. May I offer my congratulations on your betrothal to the Duke of Berenford? It is an excellent match, and as I have been saying to Lady Westcott, I think him precisely the man to rein in your occasionally headstrong nature."

Diana started, and Annabelle looked at her with some alarm. Diana was determined to be kind to her sister's betrothed, and her voice was soft as she replied, "Thank you, Lord Winsborough." Diana could not resist adding, however, "But I am surprised to see you, here in London. I thought you disliked the city and much preferred the rural life."

Winsborough nodded. "That is so. And yet, I could not help but think it proper for me to come and lend my support to the family. After all, once you and Berenford are wed, Annabelle and I shall be free to announce our betrothal and follow you down the aisle shortly thereafter."

With those words Winsborough smiled warmly at Annabelle, causing her to blush prettily and Diana to forgive him everything. What matter that he and she did not always rub together well? It was Annabelle Winsborough wished to marry, and he did seem to make her happy. For that, Diana would have tolerated far worse criticism of her behavior than he had yet spoken.

Still, Winsborough's words gave Diana pause. Would Berenford try to rein in her headstrong behavior? The thought made Diana uneasy, for she knew it was not in her nature to tolerate such interference.

Diana also found herself wondering if Winsborough had

ever kissed or would ever kiss Annabelle the way James had kissed her.

"Diana, you are shockingly distracted!" Lady Westcott said sharply. "Lord Winsborough has kindly asked if you would accompany him when he takes Annabelle out for a drive this afternoon, and I have assured him you would, but I think," she added acidly, "that he would prefer to hear it from your own lips."

Hastily, Diana replied, "Yes, of course I am happy to accompany you."

Several hours later, Diana found herself thinking that happy was something of an exaggeration. Winsborough knew what suited Annabelle and had chosen his cattle accordingly. At least that was the charitable face Diana put upon the matter. The carriage was wide and low slung, the horses sedate creatures that moved through the busy London streets easily and at a pace that set Diana's teeth on edge by their slowness.

By the time they reached the park, Diana was heartily bored and felt that she could have walked the distance faster. Nor did it improve her mood to listen to the sweet words spoken between Annabelle and Winsborough. Now if it were Berenford speaking such words to her, that would be different!

Suddenly, there he was, driving his high-perch phaeton, coming toward them. Without realizing she was doing so, Diana leaned forward, waving to Berenford.

"Lady Diana, please! That is most improper!" Winsborough remonstrated instantly. "You will stop making a spectacle of yourself at once. Do you wish to draw unwelcome attention to your sister and myself?"

Diana flushed. He was right. She had already made herself the subject of gossip; there was no need to bring more down upon her head and theirs. And it was not as though Berenford could see her at the moment anyway. His attention was fixed on the male companion in his phaeton. Diana tried to make amends.

"Forgive me, Lord Winsborough," she said. "Of course you are right. Tell me, how is your mother? And are you still renovating your estate?"

Winsborough smiled. Always close to his mother, he was delighted to talk about her and the improvements he had recently made to his estate in preparation for his marriage to Annabelle. Now he smiled with a warmth that made Diana realize how her sister could care so much for the man.

"My mother is well," he said, "and will be grateful that you were kind enough to ask after her. As for the improvements, well I venture to say that I think Annabelle will be pleased. Nothing is too good for her, and I wish everything to be ready for when I bring her home there."

Diana smiled back, in perfect charity with her brother-in-law to be. It was a smile that set Berenford's teeth on edge and wiped the smile from his face that had appeared the moment he had caught sight of Diana. It was replaced by a fierce scowl that caused more than one observer to comment that something had set Berenford's back up, and they did not wish to be in his way.

Winsborough, however, knew his duty and planned to draw his carriage to a halt so that Berenford could, quite correctly, greet his fiancée. Unfortunately, the press of carriages in the park made that impossible, and Berenford could do no more than nod to her as they passed.

To Berenford, it looked as though the man had purposely prevented him from speaking with Diana, and it did not improve his temper. What the devil was Diana doing driving out with another man anyway?

In his own mind Berenford rapidly ran through what he knew of the family. Diana had no brothers, of that he was certain, and Lady Brisbane's son was off to war. To be sure, there was no direct impropriety, but nevertheless it would be cause for gossip, and Berenford could not help thinking there had been enough of that already.

The more Berenford thought about the matter, the more unhappy he became. He had far too many acquaintances who would be happy to roast him about Diana's riding out with another man—acquaintances who might well remember Clarissa. As he remembered Clarissa.

This was not, could not be, the same, Jeremy told himself firmly. Perhaps the stranger was a family friend or some distant cousin. Even if he was not, surely it did not signify that Diana had gone out driving with the fellow.

That was what Berenford told himself. And yet, he could not help remembering Clarissa also driving out with other men. Or the way she had laughed at him when he had asked her not to do so. She had said it meant nothing, and Jeremy had believed her. Right up until the day she threw their betrothal back in his face and run off with another man. And then it had been too late.

Berenford gave himself a mental shake. Diana was not Clarissa. And no one save Clarissa and himself truly knew what had passed between them. Perhaps no one else would take this seriously. Perhaps no one else would think twice about Diana's driving round the park with this strange fellow.

That hope was dashed when Berenford's friend, Andrew Merriweather, said slowly, "Don't mean to tell you your business, Jeremy, but isn't that the lady who has laid hold of you so soundly? Your bride-to-be? And her sister? Believe you introduced me to 'em both the other day. Your fiancée seems very interested in the fellow she's with. Family, is he?"

"Not so far as I know," Berenford replied through clenched teeth.

Merriweather considered, then offered his opinion, "Not right to go out driving or pay so close attention to him, then. Not right at all. Ought to speak to her about the matter, Jeremy, old boy. Oughtn't to take up with anyone else until after she's presented you with an heir."

"I mean to do so the moment I see her again," Berenford answered coldly.

"Good. Don't want to get a reputation as a cuckhold," Merriweather said comfortably. "Now, what was you telling me about the nag you saw at Tattersall's t'other day?"

Berenford answered almost at random. He didn't care a fig about the nag he had seen or Merriweather's interest in her. He only knew and cared that Diana had been smiling at another man with the warmth that he wanted to see in her eyes for him alone!

Chapter Sixteen

❧

Berenford was still fuming when he arrived at Sally Jersey's party that evening. He had been forced to endure the sly comments of several people who had seen Diana out driving with the unknown gentleman. All his attempts to persuade himself it meant nothing came up against the memory of Clarissa.

Sally Jersey's affair was a crush, as always. Berenford would have turned around and left had he not wanted so badly to speak to Diana and been so certain she would be here. But how the devil was he supposed to find her in this crowd?

Sally Jersey saw Berenford and noted with malicious satisfaction the mood he was in. She moved quickly toward him. It suited her to play matchmaker, particularly with such a notoriously difficult bachelor as Berenford. Therefore she captured his arm and led him implacably toward the ballroom as she said, "Your betrothed is here, Berenford. Such a charming girl. As cool and aloof as you are, I daresay."

Diana cool and aloof? The notion made Berenford smile as he conjured up the image of the last time he had seen her on her father's estate, flushed from his kisses. He was a fool to worry about her.

Lady Jersey noted the smile and wondered at the cause. She, like everyone else, had heard what a businesslike arrangement the betrothal was, contrived between Lady Brisbane and the Duchess of Berenford. But the smile, Lady Jersey thought, narrowing her eyes, would argue that something more was afoot. Oh, how dearly she would like to know what that something was!

It was to that end that Lady Jersey lingered when they reached Diana, her mother, and Lady Brisbane. "My dear, I have brought someone I am certain you wish to see," Lady Jersey told Diana with a little laugh.

Diana smiled warmly in Berenford's direction. Jeremy's nerves were not set at ease. Suddenly, all his fears, all his memories of Clarissa were at the surface again. Again the image of how Diana had smiled at the man in her carriage flashed vividly in his mind.

"You are well tonight?" Berenford asked formally, only too conscious of all the eyes upon them.

"Certainly, Your Grace," Diana replied, matching his tone. "And you?"

"Quite well," Berenford replied in the same manner as before.

Disappointed at this lack of romantic emotion, Lady Jersey prodded them. "Don't you wish to dance with your betrothed, Berenford? It is a waltz," she added mischievously. "Perhaps you can complete the dance that was interrupted at Almack's the other night."

Inwardly, Berenford raged at the reminder. Outwardly, he looked at Diana and raised his eyebrows. "Would you care to dance?" he asked with apparent indifference.

Diana was mortified by the reminder and the realization

that not only Lady Jersey, but everyone present, would be watching to see what she would say and do. But if Jeremy could pass this off smoothly, she would do no less.

Diana smiled and said, "Why, yes, Your Grace, I would."

Berenford led Diana onto the dance floor, both their expressions frozen into an appearance of distant politeness. And yet the moment his hand touched her back, Diana found herself wanting to melt against Jeremy. She wanted to wrap her arms around his neck and touch her lips to his, regardless of who might be watching. How the devil, she wondered, could he not feel a thing?

Oh, but Berenford did feel a thing. Several things, in fact, including the realization that unless he held Diana a discreet distance away from his body, he was in danger of disgracing both of them. His fingertips seemed on fire from touching her, and it was all he could do not to tremble. Jeremy wanted to sweep Diana up into his embrace and kiss her as though they were the only ones in the world. But they were not. Instead, because his training had been too thorough and because he still kept remembering Diana smiling, like Clarissa, at another man, Berenford kept Diana that safe, discreet distance away from his body and that polite, cool smile upon his face.

To all of the fascinated observers, it appeared that the Earl of Westcott's daughter and the Duke of Berenford were the perfect picture of propriety. Not for them the scandalous closeness with which some young people dared to dance the waltz! Not for them the impertinence of trying to steal an intimacy that did not belong between a couple before the wedding vows were exchanged. Berenford and Lady Diana were the perfect example of how a betrothed couple ought to behave, and it only went to show the wisdom of allowing one's family to arrange these things instead of falling prey to ridiculous romantic notions such as love.

"I meant to tell you," Diana said as they whirled about, "that Papa has had word from home. Peter is driving Rawlins to distraction with the way he darts in and about among the horses. But Rawlins says he also promises to make an excellent groom someday."

Now Berenford smiled and unbent a trifle. "I thought that would be the case," he conceded. "Even to the point of driving Rawlins to distraction."

A little more of the tension eased. Diana tried again, still puzzled by the constraint between them. "Your aunt, Mrs. Cathcart, came to call," she said.

Instantly, Berenford froze. What the devil had Aunt Elizabeth said to Diana? Had she tried to persuade her to break off the match?

"Did she?" he asked carefully.

"Yes, and I liked your aunt very much. But what is wrong, Jeremy?" Diana asked, sensing the change in him.

"What do you mean?" Berenford asked.

"You are holding me as if I were fragile porcelain and you daren't bring me any closer," Diana said with some asperity. "From the moment I mentioned your aunt, you have grown even stiffer."

Berenford wanted to close his eyes and make all the doubts, all the fears, go away. He wanted to forget Clarissa. He wanted to forget his fears about what Aunt Elizabeth might have said to Diana. He wanted things to be as they had been when he was James, the groom, and she was Lady Diana. But that was not possible.

Instead, he said defensively, raising his eyebrows as he did so, "I am merely treating you as a gentleman treats a lady, holding you at a proper distance. You once said you wished me to behave with perfect propriety. Have you," he asked, his voice low and full of hope, "changed your mind?"

Diana did not dare answer truthfully, not when her heart was beating so rapidly. Instead, she stayed discreetly silent. Though her color, Diana thought, must surely have given her away!

Berenford waited a moment. When she did not speak, he went on in a light almost teasing tone, "I am holding you the precise distance prescribed by propriety. I am certain a measuring device would prove it."

"I have no doubt you are right," Diana answered crossly, though she kept her smile fixed firmly in place.

A shaft of hope shot through Berenford at her tone. He wished he could pull Diana closer. He wanted to kiss her and resolve this constraint between them. But there were too many eyes on them already, and he could not. Instead, Jeremy screwed up his courage and spoke of the subject that had occupied his attention for the past many hours.

"I noticed you in the park this afternoon," he said quietly.

Diana frowned. Was this the cause of the trouble? "I saw you, as well," she replied, eager to explain. "Unfortunately, the press of carriages prevented us from speaking."

Berenford began to relax. Diana did not seem reluctant to discuss the matter. Surely, his doubts were foolish. "Your escort seemed a most proper gentleman," Jeremy said. "Perhaps he did not wish to inconvenience anyone by stopping?"

"Winsborough? Most certainly he is a proper gentleman," Diana replied promptly, smiling at the thought. "Indeed," she added mischievously, "propriety might well be considered his greatest virtue."

Drat that smile! It roused his fears all over again, Jeremy thought angrily. It was far more genuine than any Diana had given him thus far this evening.

"So you admire Winsborough for that?" he asked, careful to keep all emotion out of his voice.

Diana considered the question. "Yes, I suppose I should have to say that it is one of the main reasons my parents agreed to the betrothal."

Berenford missed a step. It wasn't possible. Deep within his heart, whatever his foolish suspicions, Jeremy had never really believed Diana would cry off as Clarissa had done. Or that if she did, it would be to marry another man. Berenford reeled with the thought that it could be happening once again. Desperately, he tried to hold on to the present. How could Diana, he reminded himself, how could this Winsborough, simply ignore a publicized betrothal? Particularly when she said that propriety was Winsborough's greatest virtue?

Diana was surprised at Jeremy's stumble, but she went on, "That and his title and a handy inheritance, of course. My parents are nothing if not practical."

"Practical?" Berenford demanded in disbelief. He pressed on, hoping this nightmare would end, that Diana would say something to dispel his worst fears. "You call it practical to prefer his suit to marriage with a duke?"

Diana opened her eyes wide. "But there is no question of marriage with a duke," she said, bewildered.

Worse and worse! Her words were like an echo of Clarissa's flinging his title in Jeremy's face. Telling him she had agreed to the betrothal for the sake of her parents, but that she would never marry him, a stuffy duke. That she preferred a more common fellow.

Berenford did not even hear the confusion in Diana's

voice. He was too caught up in the raw memory of Clarissa's betrayal and his fear that it was happening all over again. "You are that determined not to marry me?" Jeremy demanded, not caring who saw his anger.

Diana stared up at Berenford. Surely, he could not mean what he seemed to mean? Didn't he know about the betrothal between Winsborough and her sister? To be sure it hadn't been formally announced, but it was common knowledge among the family, and surely someone had mentioned it to Berenford?

But obviously no one had, for in the next moment, before Diana could even put words to her confusion, Berenford's voice sliced through her.

"Unless you have forgotten," Jeremy said, acid in his voice, "there is a formal betrothal between us. Are you, can your family, can this man really be so lost to decency, to all propriety, as to court you when you have not publicly cried off with me?"

Diana laughed. She could not help herself. How could he even think such an impossible thing? It was absurd.

Berenford grew angrier. "Do I mean nothing to you, then?" he demanded harshly. His voice dropped lower. "Did James mean nothing to you? A lark? A fling before you found yourself wed to that unbearable duke?"

Then, before Diana could answer him, Berenford abruptly abandoned her. He turned on his heel and left the dance floor, leaving Diana the cynosure of all eyes. It was her turn to reach out toward his retreating back. It was her turn to make her way in Berenford's wake, trying to reach him. In doing so, Diana became fully aware of the humiliation she had subjected Jeremy to at Almack's. Only it was too late to tell him so, for Berenford had already left Lady Jersey's party.

* * *

Berenford had behaved badly. Very badly. Whatever the provocation, he should not have abandoned Diana as he had. And he desperately wanted to believe that he had misunderstood Diana's words. The more he thought about the matter, the more incredible it seemed that she could be planning a betrothal to someone else. Or that her parents would countenance such a thing. Diana was not Clarissa, he told himself fiercely. And yet she had laughed at him.

Berenford took a deep breath. There had to be an explanation. He ought to have stayed and let Diana tell him what it was. She had wanted to do so, he had seen it in her face. Jeremy sighed. Tomorrow he would go and see Diana and untangle this sorry web. If, despite all the force of Society, she truly meant to cry off, he would face it then.

But nothing in the world could have made Berenford go back in there tonight, not when his emotions were still so raw. Not when his mind's eye conjured up so easily the sight of Diana's face praising that other man. Jeremy found himself wanting to plant the fellow a facer.

And yet, how could Berenford blame the man if he wanted to court Diana? How could he blame him if he wanted to hold her? For that was what Jeremy wanted to do with a fierceness that was almost an ache.

It was far too early for Berenford's carriage to appear, so he hired a hack to take him to a discreet residence in St. John's Wood. He had not been there in some time, but tonight he felt need of the comfort he would find there. Jeremy had promised Diana he would not have a mistress after they were married, but they were not married yet, he told himself firmly. Nor, after tonight, was he certain they would ever be married.

As Berenford considered what had just occurred, he shuddered. Thank God his mother was past attending such parties! Still, she would hear what had occurred. It would give her one more cause for exasperation. Jeremy sighed. For as long as he could recall, he had been a disappointment to his parents. It looked as if that was going to continue. Just as his mother had blamed him for Clarissa, so, too, would she blame him if Diana cried off.

The carriage pulled to a halt in front of the house in St. John's Wood. Berenford hesitated on the top step. He had not been to see his mistress since before his journey to play the part of the groom on Lord Westcott's estate. Then he shrugged. It was the business of a mistress to wait. He rapped soundly on the door and greeted by name the startled servant who opened it.

"I shall show myself in," Jeremy said, handing his things to the fellow.

"But—"

Berenford did not wait. He moved swiftly to the drawing room where he expected to find Jenny waiting for him. She was there, but not alone. At the sight of him, Jenny instantly rose to her feet, and the gentleman with her hastily scrambled to his.

"Jeremy!" she said breathlessly. "What are you doing here?" When he did not at once answer, Jenny moved closer, drawing her wrapper closed at the chest. "Do not be angry, Jeremy. I read the notice of your betrothal in the paper, and when you did not come for so many weeks, I thought you had given me my congé."

Berenford sighed inwardly. Aloud he said, "I am not angry, Jenny. And you are quite right, I did mean to give you your congé. I just thought to see you one last time."

"Shall I leave?" the gentleman stammered, recognizing Berenford only too well.

Jeremy waved his hand carelessly. "No, no, it is I who shall leave." He took Jenny's hand in his and kissed it. "I shall send you a parting present in the morning," he promised gently.

And then he was gone, leaving Jenny to sigh romantically behind him. But Berenford was not so pleased. He had been foolish to come here, he thought as he tried to find a hack to return him home. He had not really wanted to be with Jenny. It had not been his desire since the moment he set eyes on Diana, and he ought to have formally released Jenny from their arrangement weeks ago. Why hadn't he? Berenford tried to remember. Strange as it now seemed, he had thought, before he left to play the role of groom, that the comfortable arrangement with Jenny need not change. And since he returned to London, he hadn't thought of Jenny long enough to remember to send her a parting gift.

Why, then, had he come tonight since he no longer desired Jenny? Berenford smiled wryly at himself. He had wanted someone to talk to, someone who would listen. Not his mother, that was certain, Berenford thought. No, nor any of his cronies who would think it such a rich jest to know how taken he was with Diana, how easily overset by the thought she might break the betrothal and wed someone else. Were they even now wagering at White's, he wondered, that Diana would treat him as Clarissa had?

Berenford spotted a hack. No doubt the driver had just left someone else off who was visiting a mistress. Jeremy hailed the hack and, in a fit of defiance, gave the driver order to take him to White's. Let them wager before his very face!

Berenford settled against the squabs. He meant to get

drunk tonight. Tomorrow he would find a proper present for Jenny and send it to her. Then he would meet with Diana to discover his fate. But tonight he would obliterate his sorrows and the devil help anyone who got in his way.

Chapter Seventeen

~

Diana stared at the roses on her dresser, her face flushed with mortification. The memory of last night was far too vivid in her mind for her to view them with equanimity. How dare Jeremy think he could make matters better merely by sending her flowers? And how could she have made such a mess of things last night? She had laughed at him—laughed in the middle of the dance floor! It was scarcely a wonder Jeremy had abandoned her there, and yet it was a humiliation Diana found hard to forgive.

Diana stared at the roses. She had been slow, Diana thought. For too slow, to realize what Jeremy meant and therefore too slow to correct his assumption. How had he gotten such a notion?

Because, a tiny voice replied, Diana had been seated in a carriage with another gentleman. Jeremy must have thought that Annabelle was there to play propriety as she had done when Diana went out driving with him. Certainly Winsborough had addressed as much conversation to Diana as to her sister. It was her own words, her own mention of a betrothal, that had misled Jeremy to the rest.

And yet it hurt that he had fled from her so precipitously—that Jeremy had not stayed a moment longer for Diana to explain.

Abruptly, Diana sighed. At least it was evident from the roses and the note saying he meant to call at eleven, that Jeremy had not abandoned her entirely. It was a scandalously early hour to call, of course, but he was her betrothed, and so she knew Aunt Ariana would permit her to see him. And that meant she had scarcely half an hour to prepare!

Swiftly, Diana considered the dresses before her and tried to decide which one showed her off to the best advantage. This time she must make Jeremy listen, must make him regret his impulsive behavior. For, mistake or not, Diana had no intention of being treated in such a way in the future.

Downstairs, the arrival of the roses had also been remarked. "It must mean that in spite of his cruel behavior last night, Berenford means to carry through with this betrothal," Lady Brisbane said triumphantly.

"Unless it is a final token before Berenford breaks things off entirely," Lady Westcott retorted with bitterness.

That gave Lady Brisbane pause. "Perhaps," she said thoughtfully, "but we must hope it does not."

Lady Westcott sighed.

Lady Brisbane heard the sigh. "And what, precisely, does that mean, Delwinia?" she asked, fixing her younger sister with a stern stare.

Lady Westcott sighed again. "Even if Berenford is willing to continue the betrothal, I am not certain that Diana will do so. She was in such a temper last night when we returned home! I vow I do not know my daughter anymore."

"Fiddlesticks!" Lady Brisbane retorted. "Diana will do as she is told. She has thus far, has she not, Delwinia? Diana is a sensible girl, with the wit to know how little choice she has."

Lady Westcott started to protest, and Lady Brisbane held up a hand to forestall her. "I know what you are about to say, and you are mistaken," Lady Brisbane told her sister firmly. "Diana is headstrong and disobedient and impossibly hot to hand at times. I will concede all of that. But think, Delwinia! Last night, when Berenford abandoned Diana on the dance floor, she had a taste of what matters would be like for her were she or Berenford to cry off!"

Lady Westcott did not look convinced, so Lady Brisbane tried again. "Diana is an intelligent girl," she said. "Intelligent enough to know that she would much dislike facing such snickers, such gossip, such falsely sympathetic smiles every day. As she will, unless she and Berenford patch matters up, and quickly at that. No, you need have no fear, Delwinia. Diana will marry Berenford. If, that is, he is still willing to carry through with the matter. I do wonder what it was that caused him to go off like that. If only Diana would tell us. Hasn't she said anything to you?"

Lady Westcott shook her head. "Not a word," she admitted. "And Diana is not likely to. She has always held her own counsel. Which is why I fear the outcome of their next meeting."

"Well, I do not!" Lady Brisbane retorted. "It cannot come soon enough for me. Berenford will set it all right and tight, you'll see."

Lady Westcott only shook her head and smiled wanly. They would see, of course. Delwinia only doubted that matters would go as smoothly as Ariana predicted. With a sidelong glance she consulted the clock on the mantel. Almost eleven. Berenford would be here soon.

Lady Brisbane noticed the glance and the clock. "We

must plan our strategy," she said briskly. "Diana must be left alone with him, but we must not seem too eager to do so. Berenford must be made to understand that he must do some courting. Shall I speak to him, or will you? Never mind," she said, answering her own question, "I think it best that I speak to Berenford. I have, after all, known him since he was in leading strings. Practically anyway," she added defensively. "I've known him longer than you, at any rate. And I can drop a hint in his ear while you help Diana get ready. And for god's sake, remind her of precisely why she agreed to marry Berenford in the first place!"

That was not, Lady Westcott thought, perhaps the best advice but nevertheless she rose to her feet and shook out her skirts. "I shall indeed see that Diana is ready to greet her guest on time," Lady Westcott said simply.

Lady Brisbane tilted her head to one side. "Not precisely on time," she counselled. "Let Berenford wait a bit. A hint of reluctance, so long as it is not too strong, might prove a good thing. And be certain Diana is looking her best! She is a beauty and we want to remind him of the prize he is getting, if he conducts himself as he must."

Lady Westcott nodded and moved swiftly out of the room before her sister could add any more advice. She was just in time to reach the top of the stairs when the knocker sounded at the front door. Berenford was early, she thought with some alarm. It was an excellent sign but she prayed it would not set Diana's back up further.

It was also an excellent sign, Lady Westcott thought when she entered Diana's bedroom, that several dresses had been considered and discarded onto the bed. It argued that the girl cared what Berenford would think and Diana had never done so with any suitor back home.

"Can I help?" Lady Westcott asked innocently. "His grace, the Duke of Berenford, is early and has already arrived."

At that, Diana whirled to look at her mother and her face seemed to drain of color. "He's here? Already?"

"Yes," Lady Westcott replied patiently. "It seems he is most eager to see you."

Now the color began to return to Diana's cheeks and a martial glint to her eyes. "Well, I am not eager or ready to see him," Diana said defiantly. "It will take some time for me to complete my toilette."

Lady Westcott did not tell Diana that such a delay fell in perfectly with Ariana's plans. Instead she seated herself on a chair and watched as the maid pinned Diana's curls high on her head. The blue satin gown she had chosen suited her far better than the sprigged muslin would have done, Lady Westcott thought approvingly. Let Berenford be reminded that Diana was a young woman, not a green girl in her first Season. Such a chit would no doubt bore him to death. No, let him see that Diana was a prize worth pursuing, a young woman ready to be mistress of his household as well as his wife.

When she judged enough time has passed, Lady Westcott said casually, "I wonder what your Aunt Ariana has had to say to Berenford? She seemed most eager to speak to him alone, Diana."

That alarmed Diana. She flushed as she recalled the advice her aunt had given her, the day before. What if Aunt Ariana were to speak so to Jeremy?

"I'm ready," Diana said hastily.

Together Diana and her mother went down the stairs to the drawing room. Even from the hallway, they could hear Lady Brisbane's clear voice as she said, ". . . nonsense, but a light hand is always wise on the reins. Even a judicious kiss might help your cause, Berenford."

That was far more than enough! Diana flung open the drawing room door, her cheeks flushed with color as she greeted the duke. Her color rose even higher as he took her hands in his and lifted first one and then the other to his lips. There was a husky warmth in his voice as he greeted her.

"Hello, Diana. Your aunt has just been explaining to me about the betrothal between Lord Winsborough and your sister, Annabelle," he said.

Diana looked up at him with eyes wide, as always taken by Berenford's charm. Then her eyes narrowed as she demanded tartly, "And so you thought you had best apologize for your mistake, Your Grace?"

"Apologize?" Berenford lifted an eyebrow. "No, I had not thought to do so," he said coolly. At her look of surprise, he went on, more gently, "Ought I to apologize for caring so deeply when I thought your affections might have turned elsewhere? Ought I to apologize for feeling such despair when you laughed?"

Berenford's voice had dropped even lower, the warmth more pronounced. Diana was not proof against such things and without even knowing it she leaned toward him. She wanted to tell him that his despair was nothing compared to hers when she thought she had lost him.

Instead, Diana forced herself to say aloud, "You treated me very badly at the ball."

Berenford nodded. His lips quirked upward into a wry grin. "I know it and have been regretting my folly ever since. I can only plead the strength of my emotions that made it impossible for me to bear the thought of losing you.

I can only say my despair outweighed any thoughts of how my behavior might affect anyone save myself."

Berenford's voice seemed to throb with emotion and to spare herself, Diana half turned away. "That does not seem a recommendation for marriage," she said. "How often will your emotions cause you to ignore the effect of your behavior on me then?"

Warm, strong hands were placed on Diana's shoulders. Warm, strong hands turned her around and cupped her chin, tilting her face up to look at Jeremy's. His eyes and his voice were earnest as he said, "I cannot promise I will not hurt you again. I can only say that if you are willing to teach me I shall do my very best to learn to be aware of such matters. Will you teach me, Diana?"

Unfair! She thought. How dare Jeremy do and say such things as he must know would capture her heart? How dare he look at her with such hungry eyes? Hold her chin with such a trembling hand? Plead with such a humble voice?

"Can you learn?" Diana whispered back.

Jeremy bent forward and kissed her gently on the lips. Neither he nor Diana knew that Lady Westcott and her sister watched them both with baited breath.

"I am willing to try," he said simply. "Will you give me the chance?"

For a long moment, far too long, Jeremy and Diana stared at one another. Then, with something akin to a sob, Diana stepped back and away from Berenford.

"Yes."

"Excellent!" Lady Brisbane pronounced approvingly.

That brought Jeremy and Diana abruptly to an awareness that the entire scene between them had been witnessed. Both had the grace to blush. Which was, Lady Westcott thought, a charming thing. Even more charming was the way Berenford reached for Diana's hand and she held it out to him. All in all, Lady Westcott thought approvingly, matters were moving along just as they ought. Berenford's next words seemed to prove it.

"I also came," Berenford said, "to invite you all to Vauxhall Gardens with me this Saturday night. I think you will enjoy the music, the punch, and the shaved ham. It is a lovely place."

"And perfect for a romantic stroll in the dark," Lady Brisbane said archly.

Startled, Diana looked at Jeremy and her breath seemed to catch in her throat. He was gazing down at her with such warmth, he held her hand so tightly, that she could almost imagine his heart was beating as fast as hers.

"Come, Diana, His Grace is waiting for your answer!" Lady Westcott said sharply.

That brought Diana to herself. "I, of course, I should like that. Above all things," she managed to stammer.

Berenford smiled. He smiled and Diana seemed to feel the warmth all the way down to her toes. "I shall look forward to it, then," he said softly. "But now I must take my leave. The only way I could forestall my mother from descending upon you to bestow her advice on how to handle me after our contretemps last night, was to swear I would see you myself and then return to tell her that matters are well between us."

Stunned, Diana snatched her hand away from his. "I see," she said icily. "You came to make your peace with me because of your mother and not because you wished to do so yourself? How flattering you are, Your Grace!"

But Berenford was not in the least abashed by her words. His hand was quicker than hers and almost before she finished speaking he had it again and was raising it to his lips.

"You misunderstand me," Berenford said as he pressed a kiss into the palm of her hand. "I should, in any case, have come to beg forgiveness. I only meant that had I not made the promise to my mother, I should have preferred to spend the day at your side."

"I am certain your mother would approve if you did," Lady Brisbane said austerely.

Berenford looked at Diana's aunt with a distinct twinkle in his eyes. "I have no doubt you are right. However I also have no doubt she would take it as encouragement to come and instruct Diana in all her duties as my wife and I thought I would spare Diana that. No, I think it better that I return home and take my mother out for a drive. She will gossip with friends and it will divert her mind. For the moment, at any rate."

It was foolish, Diana told herself sternly, to feel such joy at Berenford's kindness. He was a gentleman, of course he would be kind! And yet she knew it was more than that. How she wished, Diana thought with an inward sigh, she could throw her arms about Jeremy's neck and draw his face down into a kiss to show him how grateful she felt. But indulgent as her mother and aunt seemed to be, today that would put her beyond the pale. Instead, Diana merely said, in a formal voice, "I thank you for your kindness, Your Grace."

Jeremy was not deceived. The look in his eyes told Diana, more certainly than any words could have done, that he understood what she wished to do and that he felt the same. It was no hardship, therefore, to let him go. He would be back. And the day would come when they could share that kiss and so many more, as often as they liked.

"Shall I walk to the door with you?" Diana asked.

Berenford grinned down at her. "I should not think of being so rude as to refuse," he replied promptly.

Lady Brisbane and Lady Westcott watched these exchanges approvingly. Everything was progressing just as it ought, or so they thought. Neither made the least objection as Diana and Berenford left the room together.

In the foyer, however, Diana and Jeremy found not the footman waiting with his cloak and gloves, but Miss Tibbles.

"Miss Tibbles! What are you doing here?" Diana asked, staring at the governess in astonishment.

"Waiting to speak to Jeremy," Miss Tibbles replied coolly. "You may go back to your mother and aunt, Lady Diana. What I wish to say is for his ears, not yours."

Diana gasped aloud at this effrontery. Berenford, however, merely chuckled. He squeezed her hand and said with amusement in his voice, "You'd best do as she says, my love. Miss Tibbles is a terror, not to be crossed on any account! That I know from my sister."

Not entirely convinced, Diana hesitated and Jeremy squeezed her hand again. "Very well," Diana said stiffly. "But you may be certain, Miss Tibbles, that my mother shall hear of your unorthodox behavior."

Miss Tibbles merely lifted an eyebrow in disdain. Again Berenford chuckled. "Be easy," he told Diana. "Miss Tibbles merely wishes to ring a peal over my head and to spare my feelings, wishes to send you away so you need not overhear as she dresses me down. I shall survive it, I assure you. Now go."

Reluctantly, Diana left them, but instead of returning to the drawing room, she went upstairs to hug to herself the memory of Jeremy's kiss, the promise of his eyes.

In the foyer, Miss Tibbles waited patiently until Diana

was out of sight. Then she turned to Berenford and said drily, "Very pretty words, Your Grace. A pity your actions are not nearly so nice! When I think that any member of any household in which I have taught could possibly behave as outrageously as you did last night I am overcome with mortification. What on earth possessed you to do so?"

Berenford did not ask how Miss Tibbles knew. She always knew everything, that was a fact one learned quickly when she resided in one's home. Instead he replied meekly, "I don't know, Miss Tibbles. But I have made peace with Lady Diana. I sent her flowers and apologized today."

Miss Tibbles sniffed delicately. "That is all very well and may suffice to divert the thoughts of an innocent such as Lady Diana but I am not so foolish. What certainty has she that you will not treat her so in the future?"

"I have promised to try not to," Berenford replied in the same meek voice as before.

"That," Miss Tibbles said, drawing herself to her full height and using her most awful voice, "is not sufficient. I want your word of honor, Jeremy, that you will show Lady Diana every proper consideration in the future."

What was it, Berenford wondered, that allowed this petite woman to have such an overpowering effect upon one? Whatever the reason, he found himself bowing as he said, "You have my word, Miss Tibbles."

"Good. Otherwise you will answer to me, and I am not a lovesick young lady, eager to forgive you," Miss Tibbles concluded roundly.

"Lovesick young lady?" Berenford echoed the words eagerly.

Miss Tibbles merely stared at him sardonically. "I refuse to further inflate your sense of consequence," she said austerely. "If you wish to know Lady Diana's feelings for you, you must ask her yourself. Good day, Jeremy."

Jeremy, the Duke of Berenford, went. Perhaps, if he was fortunate, he could find Lord Westcott at one of his clubs later this afternoon. The duke sensed in Diana's father an ally and it occurred to him that it could do no harm to see what Diana's father thought might please her.

Jeremy had no intention of letting Diana slip through his hands. By the end of the month he was fully determined that Diana would be his wife and willingly so. Matters looked promising at the moment, but the Duke of Berenford intended to take no chances.

Chapter Eighteen

~

The Duke of Berenford kept up a steady campaign all that week. Not a day passed that Diana did not receive flowers nor a night that he did not dance attendance upon her at one ball or another. The day was set for their wedding, the license obtained, and fittings begun on Diana's gown.

In public Berenford was the perfect gentleman. Only Diana knew how often his hand discreetly caressed her back as he held her in a dance or helped her to her chair, how often his thigh pressed against hers beneath a table. Only Diana knew how tightly he held her hand or of the kisses he stole when he was certain no one would see them.

Diana ought to have given Berenford a sharp setdown. She knew it, but she could not. Not when her pulse beat so wildly in her throat each time he touched her, not when warmth raced through her at the mere sight of his eyes resting on her face. No, she had not the strength of character to stop what she held so dear, not even if it branded her as wanton in his eyes. But then, Diana reflected wryly, she had already done so when she thought he was her groom, James. As thoroughly chaperoned as she was here, nothing that could pass between them in London could approach what had passed between them back home. At least not until after they were married, she added to herself with a tiny sigh of longing and remembrance.

Still, Diana could not help hoping that Jeremy would walk her down one of those darkened paths at Vauxhall Gardens, and she dressed in her most flattering gown of rose satin the night he came to escort her. Rubies flashed in her ears, and a simple necklet with rubies flashed at her throat. Simple jewelry, but they would draw Berenford's eyes to where Diana secretly hoped his lips would press again. Her hair was done up high, out of his way, and she drew rose kid gloves over her hands. It was a warm night, and Diana was glad there would be no need for a wrap to cover what she wanted Berenford to desire.

And yet, when she stood at the top of the stairs, looking down at Berenford, Diana almost drew back. There was that expression in his dark eyes that threatened to drown her, and Diana felt at impulse to flee to safety. But she could not. Her mother was behind her and now pushed her forward.

"Go down, Diana! He is waiting!" Lady Westcott hissed into her daughter's ear.

Slowly, her pulse beating rapidly in her throat, her hand trembling on the banister, Diana descended the stairs. And when Jeremy held out his hand to her, she placed hers, still trembling, in it and let him draw her to him.

"You are so beautiful tonight," Jeremy said huskily, not caring how he betrayed himself.

"So she is," Lady Brisbane said proudly. "And you will have all evening, indeed a lifetime, to admire her. For the moment I cannot think you wish to keep your horses standing, Your Grace."

"And I do not wish to keep mine standing, though naturally, Lady Brisbane, I feel a certain sympathy for His Grace," Lord Winsborough said. "Still, we must arrange the carriages. If you wish, Annabelle and I and Lord and Lady Westcott can ride in my carriage. I am certain Lady Brisbane can serve as a sufficient chaperone in yours."

"Oh, yes, of course," Berenford said hastily.

Recalled to himself, Berenford managed a civil conversation in the carriage and in the sculls he had hired to carry them through the water gate. Then they were there. Berenford showed them to the box he had hired and seated Diana by his side. Annabelle was seated at the back, for, "We do not wish to draw attention to her. She has not yet been presented and, strictly speaking, is not yet out," Lady Westcott said with a worried air.

"If anyone asks, Mama, we need only say it is a family party," Diana replied crossly.

"Yes, but Lord Winsborough's presence will then raise questions," Lady Westcott persisted.

It was Lord Westcott who set his hand on Lady Westcott's arm and said, "Do stop fretting, Delwinia! This is not the place to worry about such things. You are making much ado about nothing, I daresay. If anyone asks, well, we shall say that Winsborough and Berenford are acquainted, and Annabelle is here as a treat. I told you it would be good for her to have a taste of things before her own come-out, and why should she not have some fun? There will be behavior enough to cause comment on the darkened paths without anyone worrying about us!"

If anyone doubted Lord Westcott, they did not say so. No one wished the evening to be spoiled by Lady Westcott's fretful concerns. No, it was too much fun to watch the other parties and speculate on the gentleman who was here with a woman most definitely not his wife, or to savor the shaved ham and punch.

Indeed, Diana could rarely remember an evening she had enjoyed so much. Mama and Papa were laughing and teasing one another; Annabelle and Lord Winsborough seemed happy to be in one another's company; Lady Brisbane speculated happily on everything and everyone she saw; and Jeremy bent himself to be a charming companion. When he suggested to Diana that they stroll among the trees, Winsborough raised his eyebrows in what might have been reproof, but Mama and Papa smiled benignly, so Diana did not hesitate to accept.

The air was warm and the paths crowded, but there was no doubt Berenford knew how to find a deserted byway. Just walking beside him seemed to send shivers up Diana's spine. There was a purpose to the way Jeremy moved, and she knew it. Diana was not in the least surprised when he drew her down an empty path and into an alcove.

"I ought not to have brought you here," Berenford said with a quirk of his lips.

"I know," Diana agreed, her breath catching in her throat. "And I ought not to come so willingly."

"But I cannot take you back," Jeremy added, his eyes twinkling even in the darkness.

"No. And I cannot go," Diana replied.

Slowly, giving her time to draw back if she chose, Jeremy drew Diana close to him. One hand slid down her back to the curve of her hip and the other stroked her neck, tilting her head up to meet his own. Even before he feathered kisses on her brow and eyes and nose, Diana's lips parted to meet his. And when Jeremy dared slip his tongue between them, her own seemed so eager to join the dance. She was still innocent in so many ways, and so very desirable! Even as Diana's arms wound around Berenford's neck and her hand stroked his hair, his arms were molding her closer to his body. One hand even slipped round to cup a firm breast, and in innocence she arched against him.

A groan escaped Jeremy. "You will be ruined if we are caught," he managed to gasp.

"I don't care," Diana whispered fiercely.

"Ah, but I do," Jeremy answered gently, even as he drew away from her, his breath coming in labored gasps to match her own.

He was right. Diana knew it. And yet the keen edge of disappointment cut through her like a knife. She wanted nothing more than to be in his arms again. She wanted to feel his lips on hers, his hands roaming on her body. But he was right.

Abruptly, Diana gave a shaky little laugh. "Yes, of course," she said. "I suppose you had best take me back to Mama and Papa."

But Berenford understood more than Diana supposed. He took her hand in his and raised it to his lips. "We shall have all the rest of our lives, once we are married, to do whatever we wish to our heart's content," he promised huskily.

Mesmerized by his eyes, which were like dark pools where she felt she could easily drown, Diana nodded wordlessly. And when he drew her back onto the path, she did not resist. Instead, some semblance of sanity returned, and Diana tried to calm her breathing to an even pace. She must not betray herself, or Jeremy, when they reached the box!

Halfway back, Berenford hesitated. He seemed to be staring at a woman in their path. She was beckoning to him from the shadows. Jeremy turned to Diana and said, "I must go speak with her. I shall be back in a moment."

Then, as Diana watched in amazement, he joined the

woman in the shadows, and the instant he reached her side, the woman threw her arms about Jeremy's neck and kissed him roundly. Most damningly, in Diana's eyes, Jeremy did not draw back. Instead, his arms went round the woman, and he hugged her tightly to him.

Something seemed to shrivel inside Diana, and she half turned away. Somehow she would get through this, she told herself fiercely. No one, least of all Jeremy, would know how deeply the sight hurt her.

A tiny voice warned Diana not to misconstrue what she saw. Had Jeremy not mistaken her presence in Lord Winsborough's carriage for something it was not? And yet, how could a ride in a carriage be compared to an embrace such as Diana had just seen before her?

Emotions warred inside her. She loved Jeremy. It was far too late to deny that to herself. She hurt, and yet she also found herself wanting to fight for him. But how? Had it been a horse that needed schooling, Diana would have had no hesitation, but this was a man. And Diana had always scorned talk of how a woman could wrap a man around her fingers. She had always believed that she would come to her husband someday as his equal or not at all. And in her plans there had been no room for pretense. Now Diana regretted the arrogance that had led her to believe she would not need the weapons that other women used without the slightest compunction. At this moment, in her heart, Diana knew she would have used anything she could, if it would only bind Jeremy to her.

Even as Diana stood there, frozen by the emotions that coursed through her, Berenford appeared at her side. She braced herself for an explanation or an abject apology, but, to her chagrin, there was none.

"Pray forgive me, Diana, but I must swiftly return you to

your parents, and then I must leave you all," Berenford said in a distracted tone.

Diana stared at him and blinked. Then, in a voice as cold as ice, she replied, "You need not bother to see me back to our box, Your Grace. I can see it from here."

Then, before Jeremy could stop her, Diana fled down the path. Was she a coward? she asked herself as tears stung her eyes. Or was it wisdom that told her nothing could be gained by staying to berate Jeremy publicly as though she were a common fishwife? Diana scarcely knew. But she did have the sense to slow her steps as she approached the lighted area where the boxes were. And by the time she reached the box, there was a smile on her lips and a tale ready to present to her parents. If her eyes were a trifle too bright, no one dared mention it.

"Well, Mama and Papa, Berenford has asked me to present you with his regrets," she said with a small laugh. "It seems he encountered a friend in distress and must see his friend home. He begs you will all forgive him."

Lord and Lady Westcott looked at one another uneasily.

"Does he mean to come back?" Lady Brisbane asked, bewildered.

"You must be roasting us," Winsborough said, blinking in disbelief.

"I am not," Diana replied, an edge of grimness to her voice.

"This is most unusual," Lady Brisbane said.

"Unusual!" Lord Westcott snorted. "It's damnably rude! Diana, what have you done?"

Unconsciously, Diana tilted her chin upward. "Nothing, Papa," she answered.

"Well, you must have done something," Lady Westcott hissed. "No gentlemen would abandon his guests like this without extreme provocation. Are you trying to ruin yourself? And us, with you?"

Diana sat down slowly. She felt as though she were made of ice and might at any moment shatter. She was cold, so very cold, and suddenly the night that had seemed so warm and welcoming held only unhappiness.

"Believe what you will," Diana said. "I did nothing to offend the Duke of Berenford. The fault, whatever it is, is his alone."

No one, looking at Diana, could believe there was anything more to be gained by pressing her. Instead, they turned to one another and hastily conferred.

"Whatever shall we do?"

"Ought we to wait? Maybe he means to return later?"

"But what if he does not? The longer we remain, the more people who may remark his absence?"

"But what if we leave and he returns to look for us?"

"Then that must be his lookout. He ought never to have abandoned Diana, and us, in the first place."

"Winsborough, you had best go and fetch your carriage," Lord Westcott said grimly. "That will occasion the least comment. We shall follow a few moments later. It will be tight, but we can all squeeze into one."

Winsborough did as he was bid. The others waited until he was out of sight, then rose without haste to their feet and began to stroll casually in the general direction of the gate where the carriages would be waiting. Diana moved with the others, scarcely conscious that she did so. For the moment she was numb. Later, the tears and rage would come again, but only when she was alone, and there were no prying eyes to see. And in her heart a core of hatred for Berenford began to form. He would not find her forgiveness easy to purchase with flowers or soft words. Not ever again.

* * *

A giggle escaped Lydia. "Was she furious with you?" she asked breathlessly.

The Duke of Berenford stared at the hooded woman in front of him, and his eyes glittered with what she recognized to be rage. "So help me, Lydia, I want nothing more at this moment than to strangle you!" he hissed.

She giggled again. "But you won't," she said assuredly. "Instead you'll take me safely home, won't you, Jeremy dearest?"

Berenford wanted to refuse. He wanted to shout at and shake the woman before him. But he did not. Instead, he let his breath out slowly and ran a hapless hand through his hair. "Yes," he said with a sigh of defeat, "I will see you safely home, Lydia. But if I ever catch you like this again, you will feel more than just the sharp edge of my tongue!"

Lydia pressed her cheek against Berenford's sleeve in a gesture of utter trust and love. "I know you love me," she said in a voice that was almost a purr, "so don't dare try to deny it."

Again Berenford sighed. He shook her off his arm and instead put an arm around her shoulder in a comforting gesture. "You know I can deny you nothing," he said. "Come. My carriage will be waiting outside the gate."

But Lydia was not quite ready to go. She shook off Berenford's arm and turned to face him. Her head tilted to one side, she demanded, "Who were you with, Jeremy?"

"Lady Diana Westcott—the woman to whom I am betrothed to be married in less than two weeks' time," he answered promptly.

Lydia's eyes grew round. "Why have you never brought her to see me?" she asked teasingly.

Berenford looked at Lydia, and his eyes grew hard. "Because," he said deliberately, "I did not know you were in town. And besides, if I were to be so foolish as to introduce the pair of you, I have absolutely no doubt Lady Diana would cry off, and I do not wish to have that happen."

Lydia pouted. "You are grossly unfair to me!" she cried.

"Am I? Perhaps," Berenford conceded, smiling at her now. "And perhaps, if you are very good, I shall let you meet Diana. But you must promise to behave if I do."

"Oh, I shall," Lydia promised with a look of angelic innocence that Berenford knew was a lie.

"Well, then, here we are at my carriage. Up into it, you go," Berenford said, ignoring the look of astonishment on his coachman's face. Only when Lydia was settled inside did he turn to the man and say, with cold deliberation, "You will forget whom you have seen with me tonight, is that clear? Not a word to anyone."

"Yes, Your Grace," the man said hastily. "Didn't see no one wif you, I didn't."

"Good," Berenford said with a thin smile. "Now let us be off."

He gave an address and then joined Lydia in the carriage. He had a great deal more to say to her, but he would do so in privacy. When they reached their destination, the carriage stood for some time before the door opened and Berenford handed Lydia down.

"I shall see you soon," he promised grimly.

In reply, Lydia reached up and pressed a kiss upon Berenford's cheek. Then she fled into the house, leaving Berenford to damn the coachman's eyes, and tell him to drive home instead of gawking at his betters.

Chapter Nineteen

❦

Diana did not sleep that night. Instead, dawn found her with red-rimmed eyes that could not help but betray the tears she had shed. Useless tears! Diana told herself fiercely. No man was worth such pain. Either Jeremy had used her unpardonably, in which case she ought simply to cry off from their betrothal and not waste a stitch of regret over him, or she had mistaken what she saw.

Mistaken? Impossible! The thoughts had gone round and round in Diana's head all night. How could she have mistaken what she saw? She wished she were mistaken! Diana took no pleasure in thinking Berenford had betrayed her.

Diana tried to tell herself that the woman she had seen must have been someone to whom Jeremy owed a duty, but who? His mother was not at Vauxhall Gardens. The duchess, he said, did not like such places. And who else was there, except some lady or member of the demimonde who felt she had a right to call upon Jeremy at her whim? Had Jeremy not embraced the unknown woman so fiercely last night, Diana might have been able to tell herself it was someone with whom he had broken things off. But Jeremy had embraced the woman as roundly as she had embraced him.

No, Diana thought sadly, she could see no simple way out of the matter. Jeremy had betrayed her. And yet, despite everything, she still loved him. What on earth was she going to do?

Abruptly, Diana came to a decision. Mrs. Cathcart had said to come to her, any time, to talk. Well, that was just what she was going to do. Hastily, Diana gathered a few things together and began to get dressed. With luck she could be out of the house and on her way before any but the earliest-rising servants were awake to see her go.

It was Diana's turn to surprise Mrs. Cathcart by her sudden appearance. The vicarage was awake by the time she arrived, and certainly they were accustomed to callers, in distress, arriving at odd times of the day. It was that Diana asked for the vicar's wife, however, and not the vicar that startled the servant at the door.

Mrs. Cathcart took one look at Diana's face and told her children, all four of them, to go off to another room, that she and the lady wished to talk alone. With a whoop of joy at being let off from lessons so early, they went.

The moment they were alone and Diana had put off her things, Mrs. Cathcart said gently, "I think you'd best tell me all about it."

Diana hesitated, then began with the contretemps over her drive with Annabelle and Lord Winsborough.

"Men can be foolish," Mrs. Cathcart said briskly, "even the best of them. But surely that is not what brought you here? Recollect that when we first met, you thought I might be something other than what I am."

Diana flushed. "I do apologize, Mrs. Cathcart."

Mrs. Cathcart held up a hand, her eyes twinkling. "It is

all right, my dear. Indeed, I was flattered. But surely there is more to tell?"

Diana nodded and related the events at Vauxhall Gardens. She ended by saying, "I think it must have been Jeremy's mistress. And no matter what his mother said, I cannot bear the thought that Jeremy has a mistress and will not give her up."

For a long moment Mrs. Cathcart was silent. "I do not think it was Jeremy's mistress you saw last night," she said slowly. "That would be most unlike him. Even if he had a mistress and saw her there, his sense of honor is too great to permit him to abandon the woman to whom he is betrothed in order to attend such a woman. No, there must be some other explanation here, but I cannot think of what it could be. Well, perhaps Jeremy will follow and tell us himself. You did leave a note, did you not, my dear?"

"Yes, of course," Diana replied.

"Good. Still, I've no doubt it will be a while before Jeremy arrives. That gives us the chance to finish the conversation we scarcely began in London," Mrs. Cathcart said. "I did not have the time to answer your questions about Jeremy, nor have all the answers to mine. I asked why you agreed to marry Jeremy, sight unseen, and you gave me farradiddles about duty and honor and such. But there is more to the matter than that, I think. You have spirit, child, and a proud, determined nature. I cannot think you would submit tamely to any authority, so why agree to wed a man you did not know? If you must marry, I should rather imagine you enacting a determined search until you found precisely the man who would suit you. Why would you submit so tamely to someone else's choice?"

Diana flushed. Put so bluntly, she had at last to be honest, both with Mrs. Cathcart and herself. There was far too much truth to Elizabeth's words for Diana to be able to evade them. Still, it was not easy to know how to answer.

"Was there never any young man you cared for, before Jeremy?" Mrs. Cathcart persisted.

Diana raised her eyes and looked at Jeremy's aunt. Mortified, she shook her head. "No, none. I had come to believe I never could feel such a thing as passion or caring or desire for anyone. Nor that anyone could truly feel such things for me."

"Why then agree to marry at all?" Mrs. Cathcart asked gently.

"Because I must," Diana said, tilting her chin upward. "Because it was not fair to Annabelle to ruin her life by my remaining unwed. They would not let her marry until after I did. And because," she added, her voice dropping low and husky, "I had begun to grow lonely."

Diana took a deep breath. "When my parents proposed the Duke of Berenford, I thought I could have the best of both worlds. They said he would not expect me to show him affection. They said he would probably even desire separate establishments after I had given him an heir. They said he would allow me a high degree of freedom and that being a duchess would protect me from censure."

Diana paused and looked at Mrs. Cathcart miserably. "I naively thought that Berenford would give me children, and then I would not be lonely, but I also thought that he would not interfere with who I am."

"And then you met Jeremy," Mrs. Cathcart said shrewdly, "and he was not quite what you had expected."

Diana smiled. "And then I met Jeremy," she agreed. "Or rather, James, the groom, as I knew him then. And he touched my heart in a way I thought no man could. I came to London ready to break with the Duke of Berenford, for James had shown me what could be. Only I discovered the two were one and the same." She paused, bit her lower lip, then added, "I have been so happy and so unhappy, both at the same time."

Mrs. Cathcart nodded and cupped her chin in her hands. "I begin to understand," she said, "and do not consider matters hopeless yet. Jeremy's reasons for agreeing to this match were not, I think, so very different from yours. Except that in his case there was Clarissa. Did Jeremy never tell you about Clarissa?"

Diana shook her head. Mrs. Cathcart took a deep breath. "No, I suppose he would not," she said. "Nevertheless, I think I shall. Clarissa was a beauty. A diamond of the first water, and in her come-out year she enslaved nearly every young gentleman in London—including Jeremy. And to his utter delight, she chose him and returned his affections completely. Or so it seemed. Unfortunately, she cried off just weeks before the wedding. Clarissa told Jeremy she did not love him, had never loved him, and had only agreed to the match because of his rank and fortune. It almost drove Jeremy to despair.

Mrs. Cathcart paused, a faraway look in her eyes. "I have never seen him in a blacker mood," she said; "than he was that year. And for the longest time he would not look at another woman. At least not one of the *ton*. When Jeremy did finally begin to return to Society, he danced and flirted with young women, but never again did he allow any woman to attach his heart or mind. Until you, Diana, none came even close to doing so."

"Why, then, did he agree to marry me?" Diana asked in painful, halting words.

Mrs. Cathcart smiled. "I collect he told his mother something to the effect that if he were to be wed for his fortune, it might as well be to someone who admitted that truth bluntly. No more than you did he believe he could find someone to love. And this way he thought he could not feel betrayed, no matter what you said or did."

Mrs. Cathcart paused, then added dryly. "Jeremy has been raised to know his duty. It was time for him to breed heirs, and this match seemed the wisest way to do so. Of course, I did not approve. However much Jeremy believed he could be satisfied with a bloodless match, I knew better."

Again Mrs. Cathcart broke off and stared at the wall over Diana's head. It seemed to Diana that she was far away in time and thought. Finally, however, she began to speak again, her voice low and soft.

"It was to me that Jeremy would come, as a child, when he was unhappy watching his parents together. Their marriage was arranged, and my sister has always been very proud that no such nonsense as emotions ever intruded. And Jeremy felt the lack of that," Mrs. Cathcart said sadly.

"Jeremy often vowed, when he was younger, that he would never allow himself to make such a bloodless, loveless marriage as his parents had. It was only after Clarissa that he changed his tune. Nor did his sister's marriage help matters. But that," Mrs. Cathcart said, recollecting herself, "I will leave to Jeremy or his sister to tell you about. It is enough that you know about Clarissa and about Jeremy's childhood. I have told you this much because I want you to think clearly about what lies ahead. As I have said before, I should rather see you cry off than sentence Jeremy and yourself to a future of unhappiness. You say that Jeremy's kisses did not leave you entirely unmoved?"

Diana flushed a bright red. Her voice was very small as she replied, "No."

Now Mrs. Cathcart smiled. "Good, then there is hope for the pair of you yet. I collect it is only that you never met the right man before, that you thought yourself incapable of passion," she said briskly.

Mrs. Cathcart rose to her feet. "There is nothing more to be said for the moment. We must wait and see what happens if and when Jeremy comes. And now, there are things I must see to, my dear. Domestic matters. You may wait here or come with me."

Diana accompanied her. Mrs. Cathcart had given her a great deal to think about.

Jeremy opened his eyes cautiously. He blinked. His valet still stood by the side of the bed, waiting with evident trepidation.

"There is, I suppose, a reason you are waking me at this ungodly hour," Berenford said from between clenched teeth.

"You asked me to, Your Grace," the valet replied. "Promptly at this hour and despite anything you might say to the contrary this morning. Those were your precise orders last night."

Jeremy groaned and sat up. "And did I say why I wished to be roused this early?" he demanded.

The valet kept his eyes carefully on the wall beyond the Duke of Berenford's bed as he replied, his voice careful and without expression, "I believe you said something about calling on a lady, though which lady you failed to specify. One might presume you meant your betrothed, but there is no certainty of that."

And with those words Berenford's memory of the night before came rushing back. With a curse he threw back the bed covers and climbed out of bed. He had to call on Lydia this morning and ring another peal over her head, but first he had best mend fences with Diana.

"Yes, yes, you were right to wake me," Jeremy told his valet. "Thank you." He paused, then added with evident sincerity, "And thank you for putting up with my moods. I've no right to take my anger out on you."

Gratified, Berenford's valet merely bowed and began to help the duke with his morning routine. He did not ask what was so important nor did he offer any gratuitous conversation. Which was precisely why he had lasted for eight years, having followed a series of valets, none of whom were with the duke above six months.

A sudden thought occurred to Berenford. "I shall want a tray in my room," he said.

Not by a flicker of his eyelashes did the valet betray how unusual a request this was. Quite evidently, His Grace wished to avoid seeing his mother this morning, and that was a desire the valet could comprehend only too well. The wonder was, he often thought, that His Grace tolerated her company at all. Still, it was not his place to say so, and he did not. The valet merely bowed and said, "I shall see to it at once, Your Grace."

An hour later, Jeremy climbed into his carriage and gave his man orders to drive round to Lady Brisbane's town house. He had to speak with Diana. It was scandalously early to call, but he did not doubt his welcome. Except from Diana, of course. She, he thought grimly, would be wondering what on earth had possessed him to abandon her the night before. And he would be unable to tell her all the truth. His promise to Lydia forbade that.

Grimly, Berenford rapped on the front door, and it was instantly opened. The majordomo was too well bred to express his surprise at the sight of the duke, but he looked a trifle harassed.

"My lord!" he stammered. "That is, Your Grace. Please come this way. I shall inform the family you are here."

Jeremy stopped him. "Please just inform Lady Diana that I should like a word in private with her."

A gold coin changed hands discreetly, but the majordomo was more distressed than ever. "I regret, Your Grace, but Lady Diana is not here. She has"—he paused as though debating how much to tell— "gone out. Perhaps it would be best if you spoke with her father."

Not here? Speak with her father? "Of course," Jeremy said, wondering what was wrong.

"This way, Your Grace," the majordomo said, showing Berenford into a small room lined with books. "So that you and Lord Westcott may be quite private," he explained. "I will tell his lordship you are here."

And then the Duke of Berenford was left to cool his heels. He found himself wondering if Diana had truly gone out or was simply evading him. Had she given orders to deny him? Jeremy wondered.

Abruptly, Berenford shook his head. No, the gold coin should have been sufficient that if Diana was abovestairs, the majordomo would have told him so. Discreetly, of course, but nevertheless the man would have found a way to convey the information to him. But where, at this early hour, could Diana have gone?

When the drawing room door opened, Jeremy turned to see the Earl of Westcott staring at him. He looked to be in a towering rage.

"What the devil do you mean abandoning my daughter like that at Vauxhall Gardens last night and causing her to run away?" Westcott demanded, advancing upon the duke.

Jeremy straightened. "I had no choice," he replied. "A prior obligation required me to escort someone else home." Then the last few words penetrated his brain, and he started. "What do you mean 'run away'?"

Westcott ignored the question. "'A prior obligation'," he mimicked sneeringly. "A likely story! It was your mistress, I presume? How dare you treat my daughter in such an insulting manner?"

Jeremy swallowed hard. Curse Lydia for binding him to silence! "It was not my mistress," he said.

"Then who?" Westcott demanded.

"I cannot answer that," Berenford replied.

"Cannot or will not?" Westcott persisted.

Jeremy did not answer. There was no point to it. He held Westcott's gaze steadily, and finally the earl snarled, "If this is how you mean to treat my Diana after you are married, no wonder she ran away."

This time Jeremy would not allow the earl to evade the question. "Where has Diana gone?" he asked urgently.

Westcott stared at Berenford. He noted with satisfaction how pale the duke had become. There was a haunted look in the man's eyes, and Westcott relented. "Diana has gone to see your aunt," he said. "I've not the devil of a notion why. But there it is, and you drove her to it."

"Thank you," Jeremy said humbly, turning to go. "I should have understood if you chose to throw me out of the house instead."

Westcott fixed Berenford with a piercing gaze that stopped him in his tracks. He bit off each word as he said, "That is just what I almost chose to do. Unfortunately, my wife and sister-in-law forbade me to. Go after my daughter, Berenford, but listen carefully. Diana's happiness means a great deal to me. If she so chooses, I will happily send a notice to the papers that the betrothal is off, and even if she does not so choose, unless you persuade me you can make her happy, I will do so anyway."

Jeremy nodded. "I hope I shall bring her back with me, sir," he said. "And that when I do, I can show you both that I mean to make your daughter happy."

Westcott snorted. "I hope so," he said. "If I had not thought you could, I should never have agreed to this match in the first place. Now go. Be on your way. I want my daughter back here by sundown if that's possible."

Jeremy went. He doubted they would be back by sundown. Not when he first had to stop and see Lydia and persuade her to go with him. But that he did not say to Lord Westcott.

Outside in the hallway Berenford heard a sound above him. He turned to see Miss Tibbles on the stairs. This time it was his turn to run up to speak to her.

"Have you seen Diana this morning?" he asked urgently. "Have her sisters said anything to you about what happened last night?"

Miss Tibbles quelled Jeremy in an instant with her glance. Even she, however, was not impervious to the humble way in which he looked at her.

Miss Tibbles sighed. She began to move down the stairs, drawing Berenford with her. "I suppose I had best advise you, Your Grace. Heaven knows, no one else is. Not to any point, at any rate. You had best do something, and quickly, my boy. Lady Diana believes you to be full of charm and wit and not to truly care for her in the least. She believes you to be so lost to decency that you abandoned her for your mistress at Vauxhall Gardens last night, and that your pretty words have all been deceit. If you don't do something swiftly, Your Grace, you will have lost your bride for good. And that, I collect, is something you would regret."

Miss Tibbles looked at Berenford sternly, and he replied simply, "If I lose Diana, I lose myself."

She nodded. "Melodramatic, but I suppose you mean it. Very well, then my counsel is to go after Lady Diana. Tell her the truth about last night, for I do not believe you were with your mistress. And after you do, when you are trying to patch things up, try to remember just what it was that Lady Diana liked about you so much when you were simply James, the groom."

"I shall," he promised. "Thank you, Miss Tibbles. You are the best of governesses!"

"Am I?" she asked dryly. "Then I should like to know why one of my former charges tempts fate as I collect she did last night."

Berenford looked startled. Then slowly he grinned. "Are you never wrong, Miss Tibbles? Never at a loss to know what to do?" he asked outrageously.

Miss Tibbles merely raised her eyebrows and sniffed. "'Never' is a rather emphatic term. I should rather say that I am accustomed to using my mind. An exercise I might wish far more people would engage in," she concluded scathingly. "Now go. It will do neither you nor me any good to have the family descend upon us. They will think me a meddler and you hopeless for heeding the advice of a mere governess. Now go and woo your bride."

"I shall try," Jeremy promised solemnly.

Miss Tibbles watched him go, unable to entirely suppress a tiny sigh of satisfaction. He would do, she thought mistily. A cough on the stairway behind Miss Tibbles recollected her to her duties, and she hurried downstairs to fetch the book from Lady Brisbane's library that she intended to use in today's lessons.

Chapter Twenty

~

Diana was playing with the children when a carriage pulled up in front of the vicarage. She froze where she stood, for she recognized only too well the crest on the side of the carriage. And when its door opened, and first Jeremy emerged, and then a lovely young woman, Diana felt an unbearable impulse to flee. He had brought a woman here, and Diana did not think she could face her. Not when some unassailable instinct told her this was the woman who had embraced Jeremy so warmly last night.

As Diana stood there, Elizabeth suddenly appeared at her side and said softly, "Courage, child."

Then, before Diana could reply, Mrs. Cathcart was moving forward to greet her guests. Diana wondered whether to step back out of sight, but before she could, Jeremy's eyes met hers, and there was such a fierce blaze of longing in them that she could not move.

Jeremy came toward Diana. "You didn't wait for me to come this morning," he said accusingly.

Diana tilted up her chin. "I did not think there was any point to it," she replied. Her eyes strayed to where Mrs. Cathcart was embracing the woman Jeremy had brought.

That stiffened Diana's spine even more. "I was right to think you would be otherwise occupied."

Jeremy took Diana's hands and drew her toward him. She did not resist. Neither, however, did she melt against him, he reflected wryly.

Aloud, Berenford said, "Shall I introduce you to her?"

Now Diana pulled free. "How dare you?" she demanded in angry, hurt tones.

Behind Jeremy Elizabeth chuckled. "Making the same mistake a second time?" she asked.

Diana's eyes flew to Mrs. Cathcart's. She drew the lady with her forward. "May I present Jeremy's sister, Lydia?" she asked Diana gently.

Diana was so startled, she scarcely noticed as Jeremy slipped an arm about her waist. The lady smiled at her and said, "It's all my fault. I was the woman you saw last night at Vauxhall Gardens. The one who made Jeremy take her home. And the one who made him swear to secrecy."

"Yes," Mrs. Cathcart said, a little sternly now, "tell us why you did so, Lydia. I am most surprised to hear you were even in London."

Lydia looked at Jeremy for help, but he merely waited with the others for her to speak. She sighed, then looked at Mrs. Cathcart and tried to explain.

"You cannot know how unhappy I have been, Aunt Elizabeth. I love my husband, but this past year Lord Harwood has changed. He pays me very little attention anymore," Lydia said pettishly. "Indeed, Philip would rather be at his clubs if we are in London, than with me, and out in the fields or hunting if we are in the country. He never notices anything anymore—not my new gowns, nor my new hairstyle, nor . . . nor anything. The only time Philip showed the slightest interest was when I flirted with one of our neighbors, a colonel. But even then he only scolded me. So we quarreled. Violently. And I came to London to show Philip he could not dictate to me in such a way."

Lydia paused, and her lower lip trembled slightly as she went on. "I hoped Philip would follow and tell me how much he loved me. That was why I went to Vauxhall Gardens last night. I even left a note at our London town house, telling him where I was. I thought he would come and rescue me."

She paused, and Mrs. Cathcart said dryly, "And he did not?"

Lady Harwood shook her head and gave a tiny sob. "No. Philip came, but when he read my note, he went back home. And I was left at Vauxhall Gardens with, well . . . his name is not important, but he was not a gentleman."

"Perhaps he thought you had given him reason to believe you were not a lady," Berenford retorted sharply.

Mrs. Cathcart gave him a speaking glance, then said to Lydia, "What happened? Is that when you saw Jeremy?"

Lydia nodded vigorously. "Yes. And when I did, I knew he would be my salvation. I knew he would take me home and tell no one." She looked at Diana. "I did not mean to cause mischief between the two of you, indeed I did not. But Mama had said it was a match of convenience, that neither of your affections were engaged, so I thought you wouldn't care. And then when Jeremy came and told me you had fled to Aunt Elizabeth because of what I had done, I knew I had to come and explain and try to make amends. Please forgive me."

Diana could not resist the plea in Lydia's eyes "Of course I do," she said impulsively. "Indeed, I ought not to have fled without speaking to Jeremy anyway, to ask his side of what had occurred." Diana paused and looked up at him. "I'm sorry," she said softly.

Jeremy hugged her tighter. Elizabeth coughed warningly, and he eased his grasp, but only a trifle. Elizabeth turned her attention to her niece. "Go home, Lydia," she said wearily. "Go home to Harwood. Beg his pardon as prettily as you can and tell him the truth. Tell him you acted as you did because you love him and wished him to show you that he loves you."

"But what if he does not?" Lydia asked, a stricken look upon her face.

"Then you will know. And without ruining yourself in the process," Mrs. Cathcart replied. "But you are far more likely to discover that Harwood does love you and has no notion that you doubt it. Men often do not see the matter as we do and need to be taught what it is that will reassure you."

"Do you think so?" Lydia asked hopefully.

Mrs. Cathcart smiled, and for a moment she was far away, remembering. Then she looked at Lydia, and there was a distinct twinkle in her eyes as she said, "I am certain of it, my dear. Even Mr. Cathcart, who loves me as dearly as I love him, needed to be given some direction in the matter."

Lydia took a deep breath. "Very well," she said. "I shall go back to London and pack. And when I get home, if Philip will not listen to me, I shall make him. Jeremy, will you take me back to London now?"

Berenford rolled his eyes in exasperation. "Take my carriage," he said impatiently. "Take it and go straight to Harwood. Surely, you have enough dresses and things that you will not miss what you left in London? You can retrieve them the next time you are there."

"Oh, thank you, Jeremy! I shall," she said.

Then, without bothering to take her leave of anyone, Lydia ran to the carriage and climbed inside. The bewildered coachman looked at Jeremy for direction.

"Excuse me, my love," he told Diana. "I had best give the coachman his orders myself."

"My love." Diana hugged the words to her. Beside her, Mrs. Cathcart nodded approvingly. "I knew it could not have been his mistress," Elizabeth said. "Not Jeremy."

And then he was back. Mrs. Cathcart looked at her nephew. "I dislike to be difficult," she said severely, but with a twinkle in her eyes, "but how do you mean to return to London without your carriage?"

Berenford shrugged impatiently. "I shall hire a carriage or something. What can it signify, compared to the need to send Lydia back where she belongs?"

"True," Elizabeth agreed. She sighed. "I do wish the girl did not have such a knack for getting herself into trouble," she said.

Diana hesitated, then asked, "Is she so unhappy in her marriage as she seems? Was her marriage arranged for her as well?"

Elizabeth looked at Jeremy and then back at Diana. She sighed. "No, it was not. Lydia met Lord Harwood and decided she must have him. Fortunately or unfortunately, depending upon how you look at it, my sister considered Harwood quite unexceptionable, so she agreed to the match—particularly as Lydia was shrewd enough to present the match as a suitable one rather than plead her emotions."

"Yes, and the result is that Lydia has more than once pulled such nonsense as she did last night!" Berenford said sharply. "It would have been far better if Mama had arranged a match for her."

Mrs. Cathcart looked at her nephew, thoughtful. "You are unfair, Jeremy," she said gently. "Lydia would have pulled such nonsense no matter whom she married, I think. The fault lies in her youth and character, not her marriage."

"Perhaps," Jeremy agreed grudgingly.

"She is not Clarissa," Mrs. Cathcart said.

Berenford recoiled as if he had been slapped. His eyes grew narrow and hard. Mrs. Cathcart, however, was not in the least alarmed.

"Don't be impertinent!" she told Jeremy sharply. "It is past time you got over Clarissa." Mrs. Cathcart paused and considered. "I think, however, I shall leave you to discuss Clarissa with Lady Diana yourself. That and a few other things, of course. I like both of you, and I should like to see the pair of you happy. But I cannot counsel you to go through with this marriage," she added, fixing first Jeremy and then Diana with her stern stare, "unless you can resolve this habit that you both have of misunderstanding and distressing each other."

Then, before either Jeremy or Diana could think of any words to reply, Mrs. Cathcart turned on her heel and walked away. Jeremy looked at Diana with a crooked smile.

"Well, that's put us in our place," Berenford said wryly.

Diana regarded him with a troubled look. "Don't jest about the matter," she pleaded. "Your aunt is right; we have made a hopeless tangle of things."

Berenford closed his eyes a moment, then opened them again. "I know," he said heavily. "Aunt Elizabeth generally is right about things," he added wryly. Berenford looked round. "Come, there is an orchard over this way, behind the vicarage. We may be private there while we talk."

When they reached the safety of the shaded trees, Berenford placed his back against one and looked at Diana. He took a deep breath. "About Clarissa," he began.

Diana forestalled Berenford. "Your aunt told me about Clarissa. She said that Clarissa cried off right before the wedding."

"There was more to it than that," Berenford said stiffly. "I believed I loved Clarissa. When she cried off and said she had never cared for me in the least, I vowed I would never love again. And for the past eight years I have kept that vow. Until I met you."

"And then I threatened to cry off, as well," Diana said in a troubled voice.

Jeremy nodded. "When I saw you with Winsborough, and then, at Sally Jersey's ball when you talked of betrothal and I thought you meant yourself, well, I thought it was happening all over again."

"No wonder you abandoned me then and there," Diana replied thoughtfully. "I wonder you came at all to see me again. Or sent the roses the next day." Diana paused when something else occurred to her. "You must have thought me like Clarissa when we were back home and I told you, that is, James, the groom, that though I cared for him . . . for you, I would marry the Duke of Berenford anyway. Why did you not hate me for that?"

Berenford hesitated, trying to find the words to explain to her as well as to himself. "Because it was so clear that you would break with Berenford if need be. And because it was myself you cared for. Because in your case there was no question that the unknown duke's affections could have been attached. Oh, for a thousand reasons, I suppose. I only know I could not hate you, no matter what. As for abandoning you at Sally Jersey's party, that was not well done of me. And when I met Winsborough at White's later that night, and he told me the connection with your family, I knew I must make amends. Had he not told me, I don't know what foolish step I might have taken. I am not proud of myself for that. And then your aunt confirmed the news the next day, and I felt an even greater fool."

Berenford paused, then added unhappily, "You were right to say we have made a hopeless muddle of things, Diana."

"Far worse than I ever imagined we could," she miserably agreed. "All of this has only made it clear to me that neither of us has the least notion of how to go on."

"Perhaps," Jeremy replied thoughtfully. "But I am not so certain the case is hopeless, you know."

Startled, Diana looked up at him, astonished, to see Jeremy wryly smiling. She was even more surprised when he drew her toward him.

"It seems to me," he told her gently, "that we did very well before we came to London. James and Diana knew precisely how to go on."

Diana blushed and allowed herself to be drawn closer into Berenford's arms and against his chest. It felt so good to rest her head there and look up at Jeremy as she waited for him to explain.

Berenford dropped a kiss on the top of Diana's forehead, then said, "James and Diana knew precisely what to say to one another, how to give and receive comfort and affection. It is only when we came to London and were hedged about by rules and custom and propriety that we began to lose our way."

Jeremy kissed Diana's lips gently.

"Yes, but we shall be hemmed about in such a way all our lives," Diana felt obliged to point out when he lifted his head.

"Will we? Perhaps we could manage so long as we make certain that James and Diana are allowed to see one another often, away from prying eyes?" Jeremy suggested, kissing her more firmly now.

"Could we?" Diana asked doubtfully, kissing him back.

Jeremy lifted his head and grinned down at her. "Why not? I am a duke, and you shall be a duchess, and why should we not make our own rules, on our own estates, well away from the prying eyes of London?"

They kissed again, longer this time. When she came up for air, Diana said, "Perhaps it might work."

"I think we ought to try," Jeremy replied. He paused, and his voice became more serious now. He tilted up Diana's chin so that their eyes met and neither could evade the other. "We might also, I think, make a vow that we shall always trust one another. That no matter how things appear, we shall wait to hear what the other has to say."

A tiny shaft of fear ran through Diana as she wondered if she could. As though he could read her mind, Jeremy said, "I vow you shall never have reason to distrust me, Diana. Once we are married, I shall give you my heart to have forever. Indeed, I think I already have. No matter what course our lives follow, I shall never play you false or take a mistress to my bed."

"Or hers?" Diana could not help but ask.

Jeremy growled. "Nor hers!"

"And I shall give my heart to you," Diana replied solemnly. Then a tiny giggle escaped her throat. Jeremy frowned, and she said, trying to look innocent, but with a mischievous grin upon her lips, "I suppose it might help us keep our vows if James and Diana were to meet very, very often."

Jeremy threw back his head and laughed. When he had finished, he looked at her, eyes twinkling merrily as he replied, "Do you know, I think you might be right?"

And then there was no need for further words—not for some time. It was fortunate that Mrs. Cathcart guessed what Jeremy and Diana might be about and came for them herself. It was a loud cough from Jeremy's aunt that recalled them to where they were.

"I am grateful it was not my poor husband or my children I sent after you," Elizabeth said with mock sternness. "Why, you would have shocked any of them terribly."

Instantly, Jeremy and Diana sprang apart.

"I'm . . . sorry, Aunt Elizabeth," he stammered.

"We . . . I . . . we," Diana said helplessly.

Mrs. Cathcart smiled affectionately at them. "I collect the pair of you have resolved matters?—to your own satisfaction, at any rate?"

Jeremy raised Diana's hand to his lips and kissed it. "And to yours, I hope," he told his aunt.

"Indeed?"

"You have told me, Aunt Elizabeth," Jeremy said ingenuously, "that you did not wish me to make a loveless, passionless match, and I can now assure you that whatever muddle we make of things, our marriage will not be loveless or passionless."

Mrs. Cathcart could not help herself and laughed. "So I collect," she said. Then, more soberly, she asked, "Will it be enough?"

"More than enough," Jeremy assured his aunt solemnly. When she continued to look skeptical, he added, "There is far more to it than mere passion, Aunt Elizabeth. Diana and

I are two of a kind. We, neither of us, are pattern cards of propriety, nor want to be. We, each of us, have a brain and desire our partner to have one as well. I think that we will have rough patches, but in the end we will suit very well."

Elizabeth Cathcart looked at both of them very carefully and after a long moment nodded. "I think perhaps you will," she said softly. Then, more briskly, she added, "Come. Mr. Cathcart and the children are waiting impatiently to dine, and they will not forgive us if we keep them waiting much longer. Besides, if you are to make it back to London before nightfall, you must start back shortly. I've already sent to the nearest inn to hire a post chaise and four for your journey."

Jeremy let go of Diana and hugged Mrs. Cathcart. "Dearest and best of aunts!" he said as he soundly bussed her cheek. "Have I told you I love you?"

Elizabeth laughed. "I should rather you told that to your wife-to-be."

"I shall," he promised.

Then, with linked arms, the three made their way back to the vicarage and the waiting meal.

Chapter Twenty-one

Diana shivered though the London air was warm this morning. An untouched breakfast tray rested on a table nearby, but Diana could scarcely bear to look at it. Impossible as it was to believe, this was her wedding day!

With a strong sense of dissatisfaction, Diana looked in the mirror. Her dress was too tight, her hair felt quite unlike itself, piled high as it was on her head, and her eyes were unnaturally bright. Even her cheeks stung where her Aunt Ariana had pinched them and said, "Just to bring a little color to your face, my dear."

Well, Diana didn't want color in her face. She didn't want to feel like such a stranger to herself. She wasn't even certain she wished to be married. Why, oh, why had she ever agreed to this farce?

Behind Diana the bedroom door opened. "Just for a few minutes," she heard Miss Tibbles say in her most governesslike voice, "and then you must leave before anyone discovers your presence."

The answer was spoken too softly for Diana to hear. But Diana didn't want to see whoever it was. She wanted to be alone, absolutely alone, until it was time to go downstairs. Since she had said so, forcefully, to the entire bedroom filled with her mother, aunt, and four sisters just a short time before, Diana wondered who had had the temerity to disregard her wishes. She turned, ready to rail at whoever had invaded her privacy, only to see Berenford leaning against the door of the room.

"Jeremy!" Diana cried.

Without even knowing she did so, Diana moved forward and into his waiting arms. Scarcely did it register as Miss Tibbles closed the door on them with what sounded, improbably, like an approving chuckle.

"I could not wait to see you," Berenford said huskily into her hair.

"Nor I, you," Diana confessed. She looked up at him then and said, teasingly, "Cold feet?"

"Cold feet, hands, and stomach," Jeremy acknowledged promptly. "The thought of my entire family, and yours, gathering to see us properly wed was so daunting, it was all I could do not to turn tail and fly from London before the appointed hour."

"But instead, you came to see me," Diana said softly, nestling her head against his chest. "However did you get past the front door?"

Jeremy chuckled. "I didn't," he said. When Diana looked up at him in surprise, he grinned unrepentantly and added, "I threw gravel up at your sister's window, and she fetched Miss Tibbles, who let me in the back door and up through the kitchen. Right now the belowstairs staff is no doubt sighing over my romantic folly."

Diana grinned back at him. "I have no doubt you are right," she said.

For a long moment they stared at one another as though hypnotized. Then Jeremy, Duke of Berenford, dipped his head and brought his lips down over hers. Diana held still, thinking that even had she wanted to evade this kiss, she could not have moved the least part of her body. But she did not want to evade this kiss. And though the thought that she wanted Jeremy's arms around her, wanted his lips pressed upon hers, wanted his hand to roam upward until it caressed her breast, made her feel unbearably wanton, still she wanted everything he had to give her.

When finally Jeremy lifted his head, he smiled down at Diana, a lopsided grin upon his face. "Damn, but I wish we had run away together!" he said. "Then we could have avoided the circus that awaits below."

Diana blushed a deep crimson and thought it foolish of her aunt to have pinched her cheeks. Her hand crept up until it gently stroked the side of Jeremy's face. How dear he was to her already! "I wish we could, as well," Diana sighed. "But our families would have been dreadfully disappointed if we did."

Berenford only hugged her tighter and crushed her against his chest. "A pox upon all families," he growled.

A gurgle of laughter escaped from Diana. "You will not say so when it is your own daughter getting married," she teased.

At those words Jeremy's breath caught in his throat. His daughter. His son. Between them, he and Diana would, he hoped, have a great many children. All of whom, he silently vowed, they would spoil with love and affection. It was a thought that both puffed Berenford out with pride and threatened to unman him all at the same time. In confusion and wonder, Jeremy kissed the top of Diana's head.

Another gurgle of laughter escaped from Diana. "What? Bereft of speech, Your Grace? I must remember that the subject of children renders you so tame."

"Tame? Tame? I shall give you tame!" Jeremy growled again, this time in mock warning.

Jeremy, Duke of Berenford, groom-to-be, lifted his bride in his strong arms and carried her to the bed. He dumped Diana unceremoniously upon the coverlet and then looked down at her, hands on hips. "You rendered me speechless, Diana," he said dangerously, "because you turned my thoughts to the manner in which children are begot!"

And then Jeremy leaned over Diana, closer and closer, his eyes dark pools of desire. Diana reached for him, not even realizing that she did so. She drew him down onto the bed beside her, and it was her turn to start the kiss. Now her hands roamed freely over the body before her. Her hips pressed against his with an instinct older than time. And it was Jeremy who pulled back, a wicked gleam in his eyes and a predatory smile upon his lips.

"Hold off, dear heart, or we shall have everyone in this household down upon us in a flash, and we shall both be disgraced beyond redemption," he warned. "We shall have time enough and more for this after we are married. A lifetime."

The loss was a tangible thing to Diana, drawing away all heat from her body as Jeremy slipped from the bed. Only when he held out a hand to her did Diana feel reconciled to her fate.

"Must we?" Diana asked, those two simple words expressing all the reluctance she felt for the spectacle that lay ahead of them this morning.

Jeremy nodded. "For our families," he said softly. "Tonight will be time enough for ourselves."

Diana sighed. "Very well," she said in mock tragic accents. "Though I do this only under protest."

She started for the door, and Jeremy stopped her, an amused gleam in his eyes. "What is the matter now?" she demanded suspiciously.

Jeremy tried to keep a straight face, but miserably failed. "You skirts," he said, gasping with laughter. "They are a trifle, er, disarranged."

With a cry of dismay Diana discovered that several buttons had come undone on her dress. She tried to repair the damage, and, after a moment of watching her valiant attempts to do so, Jeremy came to her aid. Gently, he moved away her hands and did up the buttons himself. And when he was done, he turned Diana until she once again faced him. Jeremy drew her close, unable to help himself.

"Dear heart, I love you," he murmured.

"And I love you, however improper and unfashionable that sentiment might be," Diana added mischievously.

Jeremy was about to growl a reply when the bedroom door opened, and Lady Westcott came into the room, chattering cheerfully, "Diana! It is time to go downstairs. The carriage is waiting to take us to the church! And, oh, dear God! Berenford! Whatever are you doing here? You can't be here! You're not allowed to be here! Whatever were you thinking?" Lady Westcott moaned.

"I don't think, Delwinia, that you want to know what His Grace was thinking," Lady Brisbane said dryly from the doorway behind her sister.

Berenford chuckled and grinned at Lady Brisbane. "You are quite right."

Lady Brisbane advanced into the room. "Don't come over the charmer with me, Berenford," she said with a martial glint in her eyes. "It won't work. You shouldn't be here; Delwinia is quite right about that. Out of here, at once!"

Jeremy looked at Diana. "Will you be all right?" he asked softly. She nodded. "You won't stand me up at the church?" he demanded.

Diana smiled at him and shook her head. Then, with a mischievous streak of her own, she demanded, "Have I the same promise from you?"

Jeremy kissed the tip of her nose, ignoring the fishlike gasping sounds coming from Lady Westcott. "You know very well I shall be there," he retorted. Then, outrageously, he added, "I have to be, for I fully intend to finish what we started here this morning."

And then, before anyone could chastise him further, the Duke of Berenford bowed quite properly to Lady Westcott and Lady Brisbane, then disappeared from the room.

Lady Westcott looked at her daughter in bewilderment. "But how did he get in?" she asked. "And why?"

Lady Brisbane put an arm around her sister. In soothing tones, but with laughing eyes, she replied, "I think, Delwinia, those are two questions we had rather not ask, for fear we shall not like the answers. Diana," she said, turning a severe eye upon her niece, "are you now ready to go to the church? As it is, we shall be late."

"Yes, Aunt Ariana," Diana said with deceptive meekness.

She did not, however, fool Lady Brisbane, who merely laughed and said, "With a bridegroom like His Grace, the Duke of Berenford, I, too, would be eager for my wedding day. I trust his short visit has dispelled any last-minute fears you still might have had?"

"Yes, Aunt Ariana," Diana repeated as two red spots suddenly brightened her cheeks.

"Good. Then let us be on our way. And Delwinia," Lady Brisbane said to her sister warningly, "there is no need, I think, to distress Lord Westcott by telling him what occurred up here."

Lady Westcott recoiled in horror at the notion. "No, indeed!" she fervently agreed.

Together, the three ladies descended the stairs to discover Lord Westcott and Diana's four younger sisters waiting impatiently in the foyer with Miss Tibbles. Diana turned a speculative eye upon her sisters' governess, but Miss Tibbles merely returned the regard with a calm, even gaze of her own. Still, there seemed to be both understanding and approval in those fine brown eyes, and Diana found herself winking at the woman. It might have been her imagination, but she could have sworn Miss Tibbles winked back.

At the church Diana was met by a sea of faces. There was Lydia and her husband, Lord Harwood. And Mrs. Cathcart with her husband and children in tow. Elizabeth gave Diana a warm smile that bore more than a trace of amusement in it. Even the Duchess of Berenford nodded her grudging approval as Diana came down the aisle to stand beside Jeremy. On his other side Andrew Merriweather smiled at Diana amiably, and it was as though she could read his thoughts. Indeed, he had spoken them aloud to her some days ago. If Jeremy was so foolish as to wish to be wed, then, Andrew would be there to support him.

To Diana's left was Annabelle, who no doubt dreamed of her own wedding day. But it did not signify. In what seemed almost a dream, Diana gave her responses in a sure, firm voice, warmed to her heart that Jeremy's voice was as steady as her own. With this man at her side, she thought, she could face anything.

And when Jeremy looked down at his bride, it was all he could do not to sweep her up into his arms and carry her off to a room somewhere. In all his years he had never dared dream he would find such a perfect bride—someone who would fill his heart with such warm thoughts and happiness, someone who could teach him to trust again.

At the back of the church a motion caught his eye, and Jeremy saw someone—someone who almost caused him to stumble. But at his side Diana clasped his arm and smiled up at him, and when he faced that someone later at the portals of the church, Jeremy was able to speak to her calmly.

"Clarissa. You came."

At Jeremy's side he could feel Diana stiffen. His own anger was a palpable thing straining to escape his tight rein. But Clarissa's first words disarmed both of them, for it was an apology he had never hoped to hear.

"Jeremy, I'm sorry. I was a callow girl all those years ago. I should never have hurt you like that," she said softly. Clarissa looked at Diana. "I worried I had hurt Jeremy beyond repair, but it would have been far worse had I actually married him. I had to come today to see what sort of bride he had found himself. I had heard, you see, that this was a marriage of convenience, and I was worried for Jeremy."

Diana lifted an eyebrow coldly. "How kind of you," she said sarcastically.

Jeremy drew Diana closer, his arm about her waist, and she took strength from that. He took Diana's hand in his and kissed it before he said, with a secret smile for his bride, "It was not a marriage of convenience."

Clarissa nodded and smiled. She looked at the man beside her, who tugged nervously at his cravat. "I know that now," Clarissa said to Jeremy. "From the moment you looked at one another in the church, I knew you felt as Christopher and I feel about one another." Clarissa reached out and put a hand over theirs. "I wish you every happiness," she said.

And then they were gone, Clarissa and Christopher. Jeremy felt as if a burden had been lifted—one he had carried for far too long. He looked at Diana. "I love you," Jeremy said softly.

Diana's eyes crinkled in amusement. "I know. And so does half the world to judge by all the eyes that are watching us so intently."

Startled, Jeremy realized just how many people had crowded round to watch that little interplay. One of them was his mother. The Dowager Duchess of Berenford stared at her son, and her gaze seemed to soften even as he watched. Abruptly, it became stern again. She tapped her cane impatiently on the steps. "Come along, you are keeping everyone waiting," she said briskly. "It is a bad habit, and not one I will tolerate. Diana, you must keep him from falling into it, now that you are married to my son."

Jeremy looked at Diana with a mischievous, loving grin. "You are quite right, Mama," he said. "I shall depend upon Diana to regulate all my bad habits from now on. Every last one of them."

Diana rolled her eyes upward. "A hopeless, thankless task," she sighed. Then, outrageously, for his ears alone she added, "But what if I do not wish to cure you of *all* your wicked habits?"

A smoldering glance passed between Diana and Jeremy, incensing his mother even more. "This levity is most inappropriate," the dowager duchess snapped.

"Diana, perhaps it would be best if we repaired to Aunt Ariana's town house for the wedding breakfast," Lady Westcott intervened hastily as she recognized the warning glint in Diana's eyes.

That suggestion brought murmurs of approval, and Jeremy led Diana down the steps to the waiting carriages. At least they were to have the privacy of his own carriage for the short distance to Lady Brisbane's house.

Diana looked at Jeremy in surprise as he handed her in. "Won't your mother wish to ride with us?" she asked doubtfully.

Berenford smiled. "Assuredly," he promptly agreed. "But she is settled with your parents instead. Where she will be much happier as she compares notes with them on all our mutual failings."

Diana could not suppress her laughter. Jeremy took her hand and kissed her fingertips. "Besides," he said, "it is our wedding day, and she agreed, albeit reluctantly, that we should have our privacy."

"I thought the time for privacy came later," Diana teased.

"It does, oh, it does," Jeremy replied, his lips moving farther up her arm. "This is just a taste of what pleasure lies ahead."

"The carriage is moving very slowly," Diana warned.

"Just as I ordered," Jeremy replied approvingly.

"We shall be late, and your mother will ring a peal over us, over me, about your bad habits," Diana persisted, though she delighted in the sensations that coursed through her as Jeremy's lips reached her neck.

Jeremy chuckled, his breath warm against her skin. "Let her," he advised. "Let her enumerate every failing I possess. We shall have, dear heart, all the rest of our lives to decide just how wicked I really should be."

Diana sighed blissfully and reached for Jeremy. "So we shall," she agreed.

Chapter Twenty-two

〜

The day was warm and sunny—perfect for a gallop across the meadows, some thirteen months after the day Diana and Jeremy were married. One child, a daughter named Emily Elizabeth Stowall, had been born ten months following the marriage ceremony. And one may be certain the tattle-mongers among the *ton* had counted the months on their fingers.

Now, for the first time since Emily's birth, Diana had been told she could ride again. Diana was eager to escape both the confines of the house and the attentions of both her and Berenford's families. The Dowager Duchess of Berenford, in particular, was inclined to coo endlessly over her granddaughter; sparking a similar absurd display on the part of Lady Westcott. The competition between the two had become too much to bear, and with a silent, pre-arranged signal to Jeremy, Diana slipped from the nursery.

In her room Diana hastily changed into her riding habit and made her way to the Berenford stables. There a stable hand was waiting with Lucky Lady, having kept her groomed and exercised in anticipation of the day Diana would be able to resume her rides on the mare.

Jeremy held the reins of a large, dark stallion in his

hands. He had also changed his garb to something that drew the amused and gawking stares of the stable hands, though they had seen him dressed like this, as a groom, once or twice before.

Now Jeremy quirked an eye at Diana and bowed. "Milady," he said. "Shall I accompany you on your ride today? 'Tis the duke's orders, I believe."

Diana's eyes sparkled with mischief as she tilted her chin upward. She shrugged an elegantly clad shoulder and said in a cool voice with an exaggerated sigh, "I suppose if you must do so, you must."

They kept their horses to a sedate pace, Diana and Jeremy, so long as they were in sight of the stables and the house. Once far enough away, however, Diana and Jeremy looked at one another.

"To the lake?" Jeremy asked softly.

Diana shook her head, more mischief in her eyes. "To the stand of trees," she countered, naming the first place he had taken her riding on his estate. "After all this time, do you think you remember the way?"

"It's been a mite while, milady," Jeremy agreed, "but I think I still know the way. Do you?"

Diana nodded, unable to speak, pinned by the force of his gaze and all that it promised. Jeremy grinned, pleased by the unmistakable effect he had upon his wife, and to Diana's eyes he seemed a mere boy again. Jeremy lifted his hand, then dropped it, and the race began.

The two riders galloped across the meadow, stallion and mare neck and neck, with the riders bent low and urging the horses faster. Gradually, the stallion drew ahead. By the time Diana reached the copse of trees and pulled Lucky Lady to a halt, Jeremy had already tethered his mount to a tree. He lifted Diana down from her saddle, his hands lingering on her waist for a very long moment. With a hiss of indrawn breath, Jeremy forced himself to break free and tether Lucky Lady next to the stallion.

When that simple task was done, Diana and Jeremy looked at one another, pure mischief, and something more, sparkling in their eyes. In her haughtiest voice Diana said, "Thank you, James."

"You're quite welcome, milady," Jeremy replied, sweeping her a humble bow, though his eyes danced with anticipation. "Is there aught else I might do to please you? For I would, very much, like to please you."

Diana yawned and pretended to consider the matter. "Perhaps," she conceded after a moment. "Though I am not yet certain what it might be."

Jeremy lifted Diana's hair from off her neck, drawing her to him as he did so. "This perhaps, milady?" he asked huskily as he kissed the back of her neck.

"Perhaps," Diana agreed with feigned indifference that fooled neither one of them.

Jeremy tried again. He cupped Diana's chin in his hand and raised her face so that their lips could meet. When he had well and truly kissed Diana, he pulled away. Jeremy quirked an eyebrow at Diana, his breath as ragged as her own, and asked, "Perhaps that?"

Diana shrugged, though heat flooded her veins. A tremor of anticipation ran through Diana as Jeremy eyed her thoughtfully. Finally, a slow smile spread across his face, matched by wicked sensations that seemed to spread throughout her body. It had been long, too long, since Diana had felt this way, for Jeremy had worried about the baby in the last few months before Emily was born. But now it seemed Jeremy was as eager as she to make up for lost time.

"I think," Jeremy/James said, still in the broadest accents of a groom, "I shall have to try much harder then, milady. Perhaps even go a trifle further than you expect, milady."

Now Diana shivered visibly. She stood quite still, afraid to breathe, as Jeremy reached out and began to undo the buttons of her riding habit. His hands were as deft as any lady's maid from practice of a sort that flooded Diana's face with color and her heart with anticipation.

One button. Four. Now halfway to the waist. And then Jeremy was slipping the riding habit off Diana's shoulders to reveal the creamy skin beneath. He tenderly kissed each shoulder and cupped each swelling breast as he teased the nipples with his tongue through her chemise.

"Aye, that's better, milady," Jeremy/James said softly.

"Is it?" Diana asked, her breath catching in her throat as his hands continued their gentle caress.

"Much better, milady," her groom assured her.

"Not fair," Diana countered, reaching out with trembling hands. "You are so much more dressed than I."

Even as she spoke, Diana began to undo the buttons of Jeremy's coarse white shirt. One button. Four. All the way down to the waist, his shirt stood open, and Diana slipped her hands inside.

"Better, my lady?" Jeremy asked, his own voice hoarse from the way her hands danced over his skin.

"Much better," Diana agreed, smiling up at him with satisfaction. She paused and tilted her head to one side. "I do hope, however, that you have not forgotten what to do. It has, after all, been a long time since we were allowed to go out *riding* together."

Now Jeremy trembled. "No fear of that, milady," he said hoarsely, kissing Diana's throat and running a teasing finger down between her breasts. "Everything about you is branded in my memory."

Jeremy drew away, but only for a moment, to turn and collect the blanket strapped to his horse.

"Let me spread this for us, milady," Jeremy promised, "and I shall show you just what and how well I remember. With this we may rest more comfortably on the ground."

Diana arched an eyebrow as though in surprise. "'Rest more comfortably on the ground'? Together?" she echoed in shocked tones. "That is a most improper, impertinent suggestion from a groom. Were the head stable master to hear you say such a thing, why you might well lose your post!"

Silent laughter shook Jeremy's shoulders as he drew Diana down to the blanket. "Oh, no, I have no fear of that," he said with mock solemnity as he leaned over her. "I am a great favorite with the master."

"And the mistress," Diana answered huskily as Jeremy drew her dress down all the way to her feet.

Before he answered her, Jeremy reached beneath Diana's chemise, his hands roaming the well-loved territory, knowing precisely where to go.

"Aye, and the mistress," Jeremy agreed. His voice caught as Diana tugged at the fastenings of his riding breeches, and it was a moment before he could go on. "She seems to like me, I cannot say why," he told her hoarsely.

"Can you not?" Diana asked as her hands slid fabric out of her way. "It is, you know, because she has a fondness for her wicked, impertinent groom."

"'Wicked', eh?" Jeremy echoed her words. "How fortunate, then, that is my nature."

"How wicked, precisely, are you?" Diana asked, catching her breath as she waited to hear his answer.

Jeremy laughed softly. "As wicked as you like, dear heart," he replied. "As wicked as you like."

Diana smiled then, as Jeremy proceeded to amply fulfill his promise.

Author's Note

~

I hope you enjoyed *The Wicked Groom* and have fallen in love with Diana and Jeremy as I have. Next, look for Annabelle's story in *The Widowed Bride*. After that, see how much trouble Barbara gets into when she comes to London for a Season of her own! And throughout, Miss Tibbles will be there to advise and guide the Earl of Westcott's wayward daughters. Happy reading!